I0533855

# Saving Eve

## DIANNA HARDY

Saving Eve
Copyright © 2015, Dianna Hardy
The moral right of the author has been asserted.

Published by Satin Smoke Press, April 2015
First Edition
ISBN 9780957540439

This print version updated August, 2023

Written in British English.

This book is set in 11 pt Cormorant Garamond Medium by the Cormorant
Project Authors, licensed under the SIL Open Font License, Version 1.1

Cover photos:
woman © Ollyy|Shutterstock; man © Zurijeta|Shutterstock;
wings © Pan Xunbin|Shutterstock

Cover design by Bitten Fruit Books

Satin Smoke Press
(an imprint of Bitten Fruit Books)
Hampshire, UK

www.satinsmoke.com

# *Preface*

**Points to note:** *you will find God spelt with a capital 'G' when referring to the deity, Earth spelt with a capital 'E' when referring to the planet, and Dragon spelt with a capital 'D' when referring to 'the Dragon' or the Dragons of old (as opposed to dragons in general).*

**Reminders from The Witching Pen series:** *The Boundary was created by God when he split Heaven in two to separate light and dark. The light side of Heaven was called Eden, and the dark side of Heaven – across the other side of The Boundary – was forbidden to all beings.*

*Saving Eve* is the story of what happened to Lucifer after *The Last Dragon* (The Witching Pen series) – the only character who had a 'loose thread' in that series. It's also a story that is so much more than that. The second time you read it, you will see a different story to the first time; at least, that has been my own experience.

If you haven't read The Witching Pen series, stop now and read no further. Read that first.

I tried really hard (too hard, actually) to make this book readable for all, but just as with *The Last Dragon* (for which I had the same intention), I failed. Lucifer's personality, hinted at story, and the creation myth set up in that series proved to be too complex to explain all over again, in this book's context, without losing some of the intensity of this story and making things more complicated than they needed to be.

So, the end result is that *Saving Eve* – even though not directly part of the arc of The Witching Pen series – is truly one for Witching Pen fans, and in particular, for those who had a soft spot for Lucifer, the first angel to fall.

It begins at the point we left Lucifer in *The Last Dragon...*

Let me tell you a secret...

# Saving Eve

# I
## *The End*

*She wasn't supposed to be there...*

Had to catch up – catch *her.*

Her feet, running from him – always escaping him ... that was all he could see.

*"...your light is so bright."*

A roar filled the darkness behind him, shaking everything in its wake.

Quake.

This was the end.

*"Meet the end riding a dragon through the skies of the future, not following history into the dark of the Earth."*

Her golden hair swished around her lower back as she ran. That was the uppermost part of her he could make out, both in the darkness and from this angle.

He wanted to rise; run with her, on legs, as a man, but his need sat in his belly and it was his belly that led him on.

Slithering...

*Have to save her before it all ends...* She needed to shine again. She could not – *must not* – fall with all else. He wouldn't let her. She would not become ... *him*.

What was she doing, down here, in the very crux of darkness? This was not her home.

And yet, the darkness had not corrupted her as it had him, he could feel it. She was beyond corruption – always had been.

*So, who are you saving?*

Rocks and stones fell.

He sped on, dodging them all, able to sense every part of the Earth falling before it fell, after all, he was the manifestation of every fallen thing.

He had made a mistake he couldn't remember. She had made a mistake that hadn't been hers.

Had it been his? He didn't know – it was one of the very few things he didn't know and it skewered him. He hated not knowing. Ignorance was weakness; the unknown led to missteps and failure, and maybe he would remember again ... with every new thing he learnt, he might just remember what he'd done wrong.

Whatever it was, he would take her fall.

*Should have taken her fall,* cried his heart in twisted torment.

He would take the blame. He would take her bloodied hands and her crimes as his own, for all of mankind. For everything they had suffered. And for her redemption.

The ground shook.

*Last chance to put it right.*

And still she evaded him, like a flame he had lost and continued to lose, leaving him cold, never warm; like a beacon signalling home.

Nowhere had felt like home since he'd lost her.

*"You're extraordinary..."*

Her gleaming, gold hair was the last thing he noted before blackness became a living, breathing thing. She ran into it – some cruel repetition of a moment aeons old that had him screaming in agony inside his muted form... *EVE!!! WHY?*

The blackness consumed him, even in this form – even as the wingless serpent – and he fell ... *always falling* ... as a new era rose. It was a strange kind of void he had not experienced before in all his immortal years. It seeped under his scales, into his skin, forcing a change he couldn't see the outcome of – something unique he had never felt before. Yet, this was so *similar* to before.

This couldn't be happening – *not again.* Harrowing sorrow pushed him into a treacherous second of dispersion, his mind scattering as he lost his focus.

Cold rain pelted him.

*Rain?*

A shadow loomed to his left.

Ancient terror filled him, and it was not a familiar feeling. He had conquered such base reactive emotions as terror too long ago to count. But the fear spilled into him, fusing with him.

"She's not yours, betrayer," came the sharp whisper from the shaded mass.

Something smashed into his head.

He hissed, his muscled body bolting sideways, and then forward as resolve pushed him on. His left eye felt damaged, but all at once, blackness faded and it faded quickly. Lights and sounds shrieked his birth into a new world, and with it came the pain that immortality had quenched.

Human pain.

It cascaded through him, a dam broken; knifed his body

and mind.

At least the shadow had gone.

Amid the clamour of this fresh torture, he did what he had always done, despite the circumstances; despite not having a clue what was happening, or would happen next; despite all odds: he followed her, even though he could no longer see her. Because there was no free will, no choice – not for him.

*"...You're stronger than your addiction; mine still feeds me."*

# II
## Escape

**"E**vie!"

She barely heard her name through the hammering of the pouring rain, the newspaper she held over her head already soaked through as she took cover, far too late, under the trees of Kensington Park.

Mark ran towards her.

She held back her sigh of exasperation. Mark was lovely, but for the past month he had been looking for more from her than merely friendship and she simply wasn't interested. However, 'taking a hint' seemed to be a skill he was lacking.

"Why didn't you wait?" he panted as he caught up with her. "I always walk you home."

"I know – sorry. I saw the weather and just wanted to make it home before it got any worse."

"The rain never seems to stop lately."

"It's 'cause of the quakes."

Ten years ago, a series of earthquakes had shocked and scared, not just the country, but the entire world as they rippled from plate to plate, or so it seemed, causing rumbles in every continent at some point over the space of three and a half weeks. The 'big' quakes had long ago ended, but small, almost imperceptible tremors still rippled through the ground once a month or so.

The end of the world, said the religious fanatics.

The end of religion, said the atheists.

The beginning of a new science, said most of her department at Oxford University where she currently headed up a research and analysis team in Earth Sciences. She'd been a first year student thrown onto the field to study the quakes when they had begun – every single year of her course had been involved as the quakes had spanned so large a territory – and now, a decade on, the data continued to be theorised over.

"Still? Even if it happened ten years ago? That your expert opinion?"

"Without a doubt. They were gigantic quakes, the likes of which this country's never seen. Certainly the planet has never experienced such a series of tremors spanning its surface and lasting for so long. That we know of, anyway. The change in the earth's geometry will cause major shifts in the weather patterns. Expect more floods, and a hell of a lot more rain." She left the dry sanctuary of her tree and rushed onwards, Mark at her very heel.

She knew she should be grateful for his care, but she found herself irritated at his ability to appear whenever she thought she had a moment to herself.

And ultimately, she was a chicken. She didn't want to hurt his feelings by being more blunt than she had to be, although, evidently, it was starting to look like that might be her only option. At least her brief placement at the Science Museum came to a close tomorrow. That's how she had met Mark – he worked there – and although she only held lectures with the museum staff about new findings twice a week, since she'd started there last month, he'd taken a shine to her and she couldn't rub that shine away. He'd become her second shadow.

"Do I need to build an ark?"

She rolled her eyes. "Don't you start. Bad enough I have to

dart around the doomsayers with their placards every time I leave the museum."

He laughed. "You're amazing. You're like a real-life Indiana Jones."

She inwardly cringed. He couldn't be more sugary if he tried. "Indiana Jones was an archaeologist. I'm a meteorologist. He studied ancient relics; I study the atmosphere."

"Still..." he trailed off, and then nudged her in the shoulder, still keeping pace with her.

*For my life...* Her exasperation was cut short as she caught sight of a few stragglers with 'God Is Gone' placards huddling outside the Serpentine Art Gallery. She doubted they were there for the paintings and sculptures, but to keep out of the torrential rain.

She didn't really blame them their response, even if it aggravated her. The quakes had been terrifying, and terror unleashed everyone's paranoia demon. Buildings had fallen; people had died. And for a while there, a significant number of the general public had been convinced they'd developed 'powers' of sorts; were stronger, faster, hearing or seeing strange things, or that other people were. She'd put it down to the number of apocalyptic TV shows airing every week, and the susceptibility of the human mind, perhaps coupled with the need to feel immortal; the sheer need to believe they could cope with all the chaos surrounding them.

Flags of dragons and saints had been hung from windows. Hundreds around the globe had confessed to the media that they had conversed with (*thought* they'd conversed with) angels, and spoken to God. Some had even said that God was angry, or, more mind-boggling, 'dead' – his extinction *(how was that even possible?)* being the reason for the quakes.

It was the fucking twenty-first century and human beings – *beings with intelligence* – were placing the cause of earthquakes – explained phenomena with a valid science (there was nothing supernatural about earthquakes) – on the shoulders of a deity. Unbelievable. When the fear button was pushed, the bogeyman in your closet became a very real creature.

Predictably, people had settled down when the quakes had. The rain, however, had not. It had been falling in sheets, virtually non-stop for what amounted to half the year, every year. They had just had a nine-day stint – maybe not that unusual for England at the end of December, but coupled with the recent Armageddon atmosphere so many were keen on projecting, it did feel a bit ... disconcerting.

Flood warnings were up all over the country – they never seemed to be taken down anymore. As far as she knew though, no one had yet built an ark. "Listen," she directed at Mark, "if you want to go home, go right ahead. I'm only five minutes away from mine, and I know the public transport's been sucky 'cause of the weather."

"It's cool," he shook his head.

Evie gritted her teeth. "You live an hour from here walking."

"It's no big deal."

She stopped, abruptly, at the north gate leading out of the park. "Mark," she began. Shit, why did he have to make it so hard? She'd thrown hint after hint at him about how she wasn't interested. Her right arm ached from holding the paper over her head, but she almost never carried an umbrella. Damn things just got in the way. "I've had a really long day. I'd kinda just like to rush home, alone, and soak in a bath, then watch some TV with a glass of wine and a Chinese takeaway... *Alone.*"

His grey eyes met her blue ones.

She held her breath.

"Oh," he said. "Well, if I just walk you to your door—"

"I'm not interested," she blurted out, that good old guilt rising. She was waterlogged and freezing. Her fingers were numb. She'd better not catch a cold. "You're a really nice guy and everything, and I'm so, so flattered, but I'm just not looking for any kind of relationship right now. With anyone."

Fuck it, her heart sank for him. She knew what this was like, being at his end. It was crushing, and not something you got over in a day, or a week, or even a month. In her case, she still remembered the bite of it five years on and she really wished she didn't.

"Oh," he said again, now looking more than a little lost.

She hadn't lied. Relationships were a no-go zone for her since Philip's catastrophic rejection of her. *Ugh ... Philip.* Only, in his case, he had been leading her on; giving her all the 'yes' signs, raising her hope...

*Great. What a lovely time to think about that.*

"I'm sorry," she added. "I really am."

Mark shrugged. "Okay," he mumbled. Christ, he looked like he was about to cry. "I'll catch you tomorrow." He nodded curtly, and then walked past her through the gate, turned left and strode off.

"Fuck," she whispered once he was out of earshot. "What fun that was."

She heaved out a breath, left the park, crossed the road, and all but ran home as quickly as she could.

Her home was an Edwardian terraced house in Sussex Place. She had her parents to thank for that, or rather, their passing. They had died in a plane crash when she had been eighteen – ten years ago. There had been no survivors. On its way to New York from Heathrow, the cause of the aeroplane's failure had been directly attributed to the quakes that had begun, unexpectedly, in the early hours of that morning.

It had been her fault – her idea. She had bought the tickets;

convinced them a week away having some well-deserved fun would be just what they needed. She'd give up her inherited luxury dwellings in a heartbeat to see her parents again.

She had been taking a class on the theories and hypotheses surrounding black holes, and whether black holes could actually be simulated in Earth's own atmosphere, when the call had come in.

Evie shook her head to rid her of the memories she never wanted to relive.

Her front door loomed, and she raced up the porch steps, grabbing her key out of her coat pocket as she did so. Five seconds later, she was leaning on the other side of the oak wood, warmer, but no less wet.

What a crazy few years it had been. At least she'd never once been out of a job. After tomorrow, she had two weeks off, although being freelance half of the time, she suspected she'd just spend it working. Work was sort of all you had when it was just you and your thoughts one hundred percent of the time.

But she loved her job – that was something.

She chucked the drenched newspaper on the hallway table, tugged at the buckles of her ankle boots and kicked them off.

As she pulled at the buttons of her trench coat, her eyes fell on the article at the bottom of the folded paper, some of the words too smudged to make out, but she recognised the subject of the photo: Ricardo Bellver's Fallen Angel statue, in Parque del Buen Retiro in Madrid.

The beautiful piece depicted Lucifer's fall from Heaven.

She had visited it years back, one sunset, while on a work trip to Madrid; had zoned out at its beauty, and then had inanely found herself crying in front of it when she had woken up from her daydream. What the hell she'd been daydreaming about, she couldn't remember, but the statue she had never forgotten.

Why was it being talked about in today's issue? She hadn't had a chance to read it. She'd have to try and find out via Google, because the printed text had all but washed away.

If she cared enough to bother. Right now, she didn't because her comfy, dry sofa beckoned her.

She wriggled out of her coat, hung it up, and then wandered into the living room, thankful for the gas central heating system warming up every corner of the building. She'd indulge her guilt about the effects of fossil fuel consumption on the environment tomorrow – at this second, some luxuries were welcome. She'd go back to playing her part in helping to save mankind in twelve hours. If the climate didn't ease up, it would be the weather that wiped them out anyway, not man's own greed.

*And now you're starting to sound like the doomsayers.*

Wonderful.

She fell onto her sofa, reached for the remote and flicked the telly on, then switched it straight back off when a huge clatter sounded from the front of the house.

*Outside or inside?*

*Let it be outside...*

This was a safe road, but there were some things about living on your own that irked, and unexpected, unknown noises from strange places was one of them.

There was a loud cry.

*No...*

Yes. She'd heard it, she'd swear on it – loud enough for her to make out over the rain.

Abruptly, she stood, made straight for the light switch and turned it off. Her curtains weren't drawn and she didn't want some weirdo looking inside.

*And now, you can look outside without being seen.*

Right ... because she really wanted to do that.

Still, better the devil you know. She'd never get to sleep to-night if she didn't see what the noise was about.

With a small groan of defeat, she slowly walked towards the living room window, which faced out over the front of the house. *You're fine – you have neighbours on both sides. It probably was one of the neighbours.*

Using the curtain on the left as her cover, she peeked out around it, feeling a little ridiculous, but the dark of the room, the rain and the noise had got to her. Hell, maybe the doom-sayers had finally got to her, too. *Don't be stupid. It's not the end of the world.*

Her skin prickled as her eyes landed on a figure, lying on the ground across the road, under a street lamp. And then, her entire being froze because reddish-golden wings stretched out above him.

She squeezed her eyes shut – her heightened apprehension was making her see things. When she opened them again, the illusion was gone, but the man still lay there, the glow of the orange street lamp making him look almost ethereal.

*Must have been the shadows from the light creating the wing-like effect.*

Now that her heartbeat was returning to normal, however, she finally took in everything else wrong with the scene: the man was stark naked from what she could tell. His form was bent in a twisted fashion and... She squinted against the sheet of rain that partially veiled him from her. He looked ... was he ... trapped? There was a grated drain cover over that side of the road, she was sure – it had flooded a couple of years back – and it looked like he was ... caught in it? But how? That made no sense.

*And why is he naked? He must be freezing!*

Her humanity overrode the hundred questions and she

raced out to the hallway and pulled her boots back on, not bothering with her coat this time.

Pushing her keys into the pocket of her skirt, she slipped her phone into its waistband and went outside, ignoring the cascade. If he was hurt, she'd need to call an ambulance.

*Or you might need to call the police.*

She hoped not. What she was doing might not be safe, but then again, she wouldn't be able to live with herself if she were the cause of a man's demise all because she was too afraid to help.

Not much traffic came down this road at all, and right now, it was dead because of the downpour.

She ran towards him, slowing down as she approached him.

He wasn't moving.

He looked unconscious, but... *My. God.*

In an untimely manner she should have been ashamed of, her entire self responded to his physique. In a very inappropriate way. *Christ!*

He was magnificent to look at. He must have been over six foot standing, and his alabaster skin was made of solid muscle, every inch of it defined. Catching herself, and battling the surge of infelicitous heat running through her, she refused to look down his torso, and forced her eyes upwards, towards his face, instead. Short, dark, possibly black hair decorated a countenance as hard and defined as the rest of him, and he wore a neatly trimmed beard. On his large frame, the beard suited him down to the ground, adding a rugged regalness to his features.

He looked untouchable.

Trembling – *because of the cold and the rain, nothing more*, she told herself – she knelt by his right side and lost the fight with her good self. She looked down past his torso. Well, she *had* to to see if he was hurt; it's not like she *couldn't* look.

His penis lay thick and heavy in a nest of dense, black curls, and yes, it matched the rest of him.

She had to resist the urge to reach out and touch it. Warmth rose to her cheeks. What the fuck was wrong with her? She wasn't sixteen!

Continuing further down his body, she finally saw the cause of his strange position: his right leg, up to the knee, and right hand, were caught in the grating of the drain cover. She grimaced. How in the hell he'd managed this was beyond her. The space between each metal bar was far too small, and blood coated the area below his knee, streaming down his leg trapped below the ground. Surely his bones were broken?

His right wrist was not cut in the same way, but where the bars squeezed around it, it swelled purple.

"Hey!" she yelled at him. "You awake?"

No reply.

Her mind boggled. She couldn't fathom how he'd ended up like this. Images rose of him crawling up from underneath the road, squeezing his way through the drain cover, but getting caught at the last second... Or falling from the sky, the force of the fall wedging his leg and arm in the drain cover. Both images were nonsensical, and neither explained how he'd *fit* through the bars in the first place. Surely it could only be through force. *Maybe this is a stag night gone wrong.*

Although, anyone managing to play this kind of practical 'joke' on this beast of a man was an extremely hard thing to envision. He looked like he might be able to rip most people to shreds.

She glanced at his chest. It was hard to tell with the rain beating down on him, but it looked like it was moving. *Yes, he's definitely breathing.*

"Hey!" she yelled again.

Nothing.

She scampered around to his left side and winced when she saw a deep cut, and bruising on that side of his face, up near his hairline and along his temple, the cut leading into his eye. The rain had washed most of the blood away, but it looked lethal.

*Someone assaulted him – crime. This is to do with drugs or something.*

She snapped back to her senses, brought her phone out and dialled 999. She barely heard herself reel out all the information to the person at the other end. Instead, a strange sense of familiarity and sorrow washed over her ... and a heavy, dark burden she couldn't place. Tears filled her eyes.

"There'll be an ambulance with you in five minutes – stay on the line."

"Okay," she replied, and then she put the phone down on the cement beneath her, hoping the water wouldn't destroy it, and crawled forward until she was looking straight down into the man's face.

He was beautiful. Hypnotically so. Tearing her eyes away from him was proving idiotically difficult. She wished she could see the colour of his eyes.

Be careful what you wish for. She let out a yelp of surprise when his lids snapped open.

Before she could blink, he caught her face and hair in his left hand in a vice-like grip, twisting her downwards. She couldn't pull away, he was far too strong.

He stopped when her nose was an inch away from his.

Coal black. That was the colour of his eyes – the colour of the darkest midnight, although she swore, at this close distance, she could see flecks of gold reflecting in his irises. It wasn't just fear at his sudden actions that took her breath away. Everything about him was unparalleled.

"Eve..." he choked out, hoarse.

Shock held her still and the fear escalated, right along with a burn that had no right to dominate her body at this second. *He knows my name! How does he know my name?*

Although, most people called her Evie. Only her parents had ever called her Eve.

She reached up to grasp his wrist and pull his hand from her face. It was a mistake. As soon as her fingers touched his skin, a bolt of static electricity shot through her, even though everything in her scientific mind told her such physics wasn't possible in this environment, on this road, under this rain.

He looked more terrified than her, and something inside her heart broke. Those earlier tears slipped from her eyes.

"Stay," he whispered. "Don't leave me again."

How did she reply when she had no clue what he was talking about? He was mistaken. He didn't know her – he thought she was someone else. She sure as hell would've remembered if she'd met him before.

But telling him that seemed wrong in his fragile state. He was injured, perhaps badly. Bursting his bubble might be enough to dash his hope and push him into a dark place he couldn't come back from.

So, caught in his grip, waiting for the sound of sirens, and with water dripping from her hair onto his face, she found herself uttering a promise she didn't know if she could keep...

"I won't."

~*~

"I won't."

Music to his ears.

Light to his soul.

*Thank the heavens. Thank creation. Thank her.*

She never made promises she couldn't keep. Never.

*I've found her.*

A shadow loomed to his left. *That* shadow. *No...*

*"And you'll lose her again,"* it hissed. *"She's not yours."*

*No!* But breath was slipping from him. His head pounded, his chest felt crushed, his leg was on fire and his right arm was numb.

With his left hand, he held her as tight as he could.

Her.

Who?

*"You will forget her."*

*NO!* She was everything.

*"Then, you will forget everything."*

God, no.

*"There is no God. There is nothing."*

Blue eyes stared down at him – so kind – and hair that hung a dull mid-brown in the rain, that he knew to be golden-blonde in the sun.

But who...?

He couldn't remember who that hair and those eyes belonged to, and his vision was fading.

*I have to save her.*

But he couldn't remember who he had to save either, or why.

His will was strong, and with everything he had left, he pushed himself to remember ... but all at once, he couldn't even remember what it was he was supposed to remember.

As all faded to black, it was this stranger's words alone that kept him afloat. He wrapped the essence of her words around himself, hoping with all his might he wouldn't forget them either. Fear lanced through him, cold and brutal, when he realised he couldn't remember his name; himself; who he was; what he was for...

This kind woman felt his torment – she must have – for she

gave him one last gift before he drifted away; a repeat of what she'd said earlier, only with greater certainty in her voice, even though she couldn't really mean it since they didn't know each other at all… "I won't leave you."

# III
## *Found*

"**A**ny luck with the missing persons reports?"

"None."

"And the police haven't got any leads?"

"Nope."

"Well, he's got to be someone."

*Two male voices.*

"Did you speak to the woman who came in with him?"

"Three times. She found him outside her house in his birthday suit – no ID. She has no idea who he is."

"Huh ... from the way she's been hovering I would have thought she was the girlfriend, or a relative."

"She feels responsible because she made the call."

*What the hell is going on?*

Pain was the first thing he felt. Everywhere.

"Hey, hey, look ... he just moved."

A grunt from one of the men. "I'm almost done anyway. All his vitals look good. Low iron count, though."

"He lost some blood."

"Not enough to warrant *this* result. If this was fiction, I'd say he'd been drained by a vampire."

And now a snort. "There are only three wounds on him. And no bite marks," the voice gibed.

Blurry light hurt his eyes. His left one didn't seem to be working properly ... or maybe it was covered with something?

"Yeah ... we don't know what happened *before* he ended up moulded to that grate. Anyone got any theories on that yet?"

"No. But we might find out more soon... Sir? Mister? You're in the ICU department, in St Mary's Hospital, in Paddington. And you're safe. Do you understand?"

*Understand?*

"Can you speak? Say anything? Maybe just nod your head a bit if you can hear us."

*Are they talking to me?*

Before he could do anything, his right eyelid was lifted and a light shone directly into his pupil. He hissed and flung his head to one side, squeezing his lids shut as he did so.

"Nothing wrong with that reaction," chuckled one of them.

Was something funny? He was failing to find the humour. And now his head throbbed, as if he had a migraine.

*St Mary's Hospital.* They were ... doctors? So, he was ill?

"Don't worry about your left eye. You've got a nasty cut leading into it, but the eye itself is undamaged – we just need the skin around it to heal, which is the reason for the bandage across it. I'm Dr Strobel, and my colleague here is Dr Reem. Can you tell us your name?"

There was a long pause as he slowly opened his eyes again – the good one, anyway – the bulbs on the ceiling a little less blurry this time, and a little more bearable. He heard himself breathing – a ragged sound. "Name?" he muttered. At least, he thought the question came from him. His voice sounded disconcertingly unfamiliar. He should know his own voice, right?

"Yes. What's your name?"

Finally, he let his gaze fall directly on the closest of the two doctors – *Dr Strobel?* – until the edges of his body became completely unblurred.

"Sir?"

Somewhere beneath the surface, there was a faint sense of panic. But it was muted by the oddness of everything he felt. "It's ... er ... my name – it's..." The panic shrieked above the muteness just a little. "I don't know."

"You don't know?"

Slowly, he shook his head, his voice still achingly strange to his own ears. "I don't know my name."

"Do you mean, you don't remember? Or do you mean, you've never known it?"

He frowned. Thinking was taking quite a bit of effort, and it was energy he didn't feel he had. What was wrong with him? Why was he in a hospital? Why did everything hurt so fucking much? "I ... I think I don't remember."

But if he didn't remember, he wouldn't know if he'd never known it. He had no strength to get that out. Probably just as well. 'Smart-arse' wasn't the best personality trait when you had to rely on others for your well-being.

"Do you remember anything?"

Well, 'anything' had a pretty broad spectrum, didn't it? "Words?" he offered, because it was the only thing he knew for sure right now: he was talking, therefore he must remember words.

"Right." Both doctors looked at him quizzically. "Do you remember what happened before you woke up in here just a couple of minutes ago?"

He searched for the memory with his mind. Nothing. "No." And it was a bizarre sensation to have that panic sitting there in a dull, suppressed fashion, because he knew he *should* be feeling full-blown fear, yet how could fear exist in totality if you couldn't remember what to be afraid of?

"What do you do for a living, Mr...?" Dr Reem let that sentence trail off. Perhaps he'd phrased it as such to jog the memory of his name. It didn't work.

"I don't know."

The two medics now exchanged a look between them. He didn't have to remember anything to interpret *that* little gem. It didn't bode well.

Strobel turned back to him and smiled what he obviously thought was a reassuring smile. "Don't worry – it's not uncommon for this to happen after a traumatic event. Memories almost always return, and often sooner than people expect."

*Traumatic?*

"We've been calling you Lucky," he continued, "because you were. You were found practically embedded in a large, iron gulley."

"A what?"

"A drain grill. You were caught *in* it – looked like a bit of a freak accident. The fire brigade had to literally cut it off you, and that was a task and a half, let me tell you."

He let that information sink in.

"You have a swollen knee cap, a sprained wrist, concussion, and the whole of London's emergency services baffled as to how you became stuck in an iron drain grill in the first place, and secondly, how on earth your bones aren't broken."

"Bendy bones," came Dr Reem's sardonic reply. These two were like fucking Jekyll and Hyde.

"Jekyll and Hyde."

"I beg your pardon."

"I remember Jekyll and Hyde."

They both raised their brows and exchanged yet more glances. "It's a start. A small one, but a start. Can you remember anything about *yourself*, though? At all?"

Himself. He tried – he really, fucking did, but there was nothing there, just an infinite gap. "No."

After a pause, Dr Reem sucked in a breath signalling a completion. To this conversation, he guessed. "Alrighty then ... have a little rest. Don't, er, force yourself to think too much – things will come back to you when you're ready – and we shall return a bit later. Don't try to get up. You might not have any broken bones, but your knee's still in bad shape – doubt you'll be able to bend it – we'll see if we can get the physio in tomorrow to help you move around."

Rest. He didn't want to rest, god damn it, he'd been laid up on his back for ... how long? He didn't know. "What's the time?"

"Oh..." Strobel looked at his watch. "Almost 4 p.m. and today's the 17th December. You were brought in last night, just before ten."

He'd been here a whole day.

He faltered, when he caught the doctor staring at him intently. "What?" he asked, curtly. He felt like a fucking lab rat.

"Do you know what year it is?"

*Shit.* He drew in a deep breath and ground his teeth. "No."

"2021."

The doctor continued to stare at him in that uncomfortable way, but '2021' meant nothing to him. He shrugged in reply.

"Right, then," nodded Dr Reem. "Catch you later."

"Bye, Lucky," waved Strobel, cheerfully, and then he was left alone in the corner of the ward.

The quiet, rhythmic beeping of various machines became the main point of his awareness, his mind a blank canvas he couldn't morph into any specific picture.

How odd it was to remember random things about everything else, but nothing about himself. *Maybe you don't exist,* threw out his mind.

And maybe none of this was real. In fact, it did all have a rather *surreal* quality about it. He might well be dreaming.

He looked around the ward, half-waiting to wake up ... again.

The man to his right coughed, his eyes closed, his head turning as if he wanted to rise into consciousness, but the weight of his medication held him down.

He frowned, perturbed by his thought. Surely it was the patient's illness weighing him down, not the medication.

But to his disconcertion, he found himself sifting through and compartmentalising all the odours he could decipher as he breathed in.

*Metallic* was the overall aroma of this ward, and it was definitely the man's medication he could make out – layers of it – about six or seven different types surrounding him like a halo. The scent of his illness lay faint, beneath it all, bass notes without a voice to sound them; muffled by the cacophony shrouding it.

*Jesus Christ, you're insane!*

He *had* to be! Who in their right mind could smell an illness? Perhaps where he really belonged was in an institution. Perhaps the reason he could remember nothing was linked to some chronic mental health problem he had.

Unable to help himself, and despite the conflict going on within, he bent his head down and gave himself a sniff.

*Crackpot.*

He could smell his own medication – four different types – but no illness.

*Certifiably insane.*

Nope – not even a trace of an illness on him, although the now growing tinge of the chemicals was beginning to make him feel queasy.

Examining what he could see of his body, he spied a needle

in the vein of his left wrist; a divider connected to it, with two tubes pumping god-knew-what into it.

His right hand was bandaged because of his messed up wrist, but he could still move his fingers, albeit painfully.

He reached across and, with a wince, pulled the needle out.

*You're not supposed to do that. It's bound to be important. What if you die?*

Strangely – although not really as strange as anything else in his current situation – the thought of his dying was not something that fazed him.

*Were you suicidal in the life you can't remember?*

He didn't *feel* suicidal. The thought of taking a knife or rope to his throat was certainly not appealing. He didn't have a sense of not wanting to live. Rather, 'death' seemed a little like an illusion, or something that belonged in stories – nothing he had to be worried about anyway.

*Delusional ... you have delusions of grandeur – part of your mental illness.*

Some ... 'aura' – that was the only word he could think of to describe it – caught his attention from the other side of the ward. The aura belonged to a lady, perhaps in her mid-fifties, and she had very little time left.

*You can't know that.*

But he did. He knew it. Goosebumps raced up and down his body, and he appreciated the sensation – it made him feel like he might belong here after all in this form; in this skin.

The lady lay still, the machine on her left proving to all that she did have a heartbeat and that it was steady, but he knew better. A whole act played out before him above where she lay and he realised he was seeing her life; her hopes, dreams, wishes and fears.

Startled, he whipped his head around to gage everyone else's reaction. Everyone was either asleep, unconscious, or simply not well enough to care. *Or maybe they can't see what you see...*

Oh, fuck – he was seeing things.

He turned back towards her. Sure enough, a myriad of images swirled around above her, like a show on some TV screen going at a thousand frames per second, but he could somehow read each one.

Shock fought with addictive intrigue, but his witness to her deterioration was not the cause of the shock. It was the growing buzz throughout his body as he—*fuck—responded* to her demise.

He tingled all over, and a dangerous heat filled him below his abdomen.

Again, he looked around him, this time cautiously. This wasn't a reaction he was going to be confessing to the doctors any time soon. *What the hell is wrong with me?*

Maybe it wasn't what it felt like.

He tentatively lifted his bed sheet and looked under it, past his waistline.

It was *definitely* what it felt like. That was *not* a small bulge under the white gown they'd dressed him in. With a start, he realised he had no idea what he looked like. At all.

He shifted the fabric to one side and *voilà*! His alien cock – alien to him, anyway – stuck out from a mass of dark curls, through the gown's slit. Was his hair the same, dark colour? His eyes?

A sigh escaped the woman opposite. The machine still beeped, but her astral body had begun to reach up, semi-clawing at the air, her head thrown back in what one might perceive as painful ecstasy if they ... *if they were as deranged as you.*

His eyes raced around the room again. No one else could see this. Jesus, he had to get out of here.

He made to move himself off the bed, forgetting his condition until he wailed in agony through gritted teeth. His right knee was, indeed, mangled, just like the doctors had said. He couldn't move it an inch without feeling like it might rip right off his body.

His dick, however, had ideas of its own: it was now completely stiff with the woman's demise, as if it lusted after her struggle.

Beads of sweat tickled his top lip.

*Serial killer ... maybe you're a serial killer*, laughed his mind, displaying no mercy. They had all kinds of odd, abnormal responses like this, didn't they? Was that a memory? Did he remember reading that in psychology books or something?

His member pulsed and ached over the woman's etheric search for her salvation, every movement of hers – every throaty sound for breath she made – getting him harder, as if her release would somehow be his.

She gasped deeply, and loudly this time, and *now* the machines sounded her heart's new pattern for all to hear. Fuck it, he didn't want anyone catching him like this, tenting his sheet like a goddamned teepee.

*Ssshhhhh! Shut up!* he silently screamed at the monitor.

It did.

It fell silent.

So did he.

*Coincidence.* He had *not* just made that happen – that wasn't possible.

*Neither is anything you're witnessing.*

No time to think about that, though. The lady's breathing was growing more rasping. He should call someone in. Someone might be able to save her.

But she didn't *want* to be saved – she was ready to go. He could see that as clearly as he could see the outline of his outrageous erection, and his hard-on became the centre of his fucked-up universe, traversing a scorching fire he had no control over, but could simply not ignore.

Because he had no idea what to do – or perhaps because he *was* mentally unstable – he did the unthinkable. He reached under his bedsheet with his good hand and grabbed the base of his cock, his intention being to alleviate the pressure, but it felt too damned good, and ... something else. Something else he couldn't place.

He groaned without meaning to, thankful no one else seemed to hear it – or seemed to notice anything – and squeezed his hand up the length of his penis. *Oh, Christ...*

The lady gasped again, writhing slightly, her chest rising and falling unsteadily, and above her she practically glowed. *Her true self.*

Wholeness.

That's what she was reaching for – the bit that made her life complete so she could move on. Some people never reached it on dying, becoming ghosts trapped in this world until they got another chance.

And what on earth was he thinking? Where were these thoughts coming from? Although they didn't seem like 'thoughts' – they seemed like simply 'knowing'.

He pumped himself a little harder, setting the steadiness in his rhythm she was trying to reach and trying not to make a damn sound as he did so.

The spot behind his navel burned.

He focused his eyes on her, witnessing her beautiful ... *growth*. Because that's what was happening: she was growing, restructuring herself; a vision of pure vulnerability, yet completely unbreakable. *This is immortality.*

And he needed it as much as she.

As her struggle reached its crux, so did he, one wave they

both needed to conquer.

Then suddenly, her ghostly self turned to him.

Their eyes locked. He almost came.

He also stilled; disgust, terror, and somewhere beneath all that, a well of graceful compassion taking over him.

*"Help me,"* she whispered, directly to him. *"Before they come."*

He knew exactly what to do.

He kept his eyes trained on her, as she aimed hers to the heavens. She was going to make it, she was. He'd make sure of it.

Deep sorrow stirred for the briefest of seconds... *Everyone makes it, except you.*

He pushed the confounding sadness to one side and concentrated on her.

He could feel their temporary connection through her dying, between that burn behind his navel and hers. His cock strained as he stroked himself towards release, knowing his would be hers; gritted his teeth, all sensation now turning to pleasure, and none of it was devoid of love. Not romantic love, but the love that encompassed all.

The woman's 'glow' became both smaller and brighter as she stretched with all her being, upwards and outwards, and beyond anything tangible. *So fucking erotic...*

Seed surged up his shaft, his energy all for her, but their pleasure shared.

With a final gasp, she died.

Her spirit sort of 'pinged' from her body as it released itself, and he followed suit in a much less ethereal fashion, groaning against his closed lips as he came into his hand under his sheet.

*Holy fuck.*

There were no words. No words at all, except...

Her rising spirit brushed over his skin, creating a slight

breeze he was sure only he could feel. *"Thank you,"* it rippled across him, and then 'something' seeped into him.

It felt a bit like post-coital bliss, but it *seeped* into him like a living thing.

Her machine came back to life, shrieking a flatline.

Glancing around him, half-panicked, he spied a small box of tissues on the mobile tray-table next to him. Reaching over, forcing the fingers of his swollen hand to work, he grabbed a whole bunch of them.

*Act normal.*

Doctors and nurses rushed into the room, none of them paying the slightest bit of attention to him, so he did his best to clean himself up without looking like he'd just orgasmed over someone's death.

Reality crashed down on him.

He felt a little sick.

*You did, didn't you? That's what you just did.*

With the new buzz in the room bringing everything back down to earth, he couldn't quite capture the essence of what had actually taken place, although he remembered what he'd seen and what he'd heard her say. *Insane...*

Or perhaps he wasn't.

Perhaps he wasn't quite ready for the loony bin yet, for all at once, he realised something – something, not to do with his mental state of health, but with the state of his physical body.

Expecting the worst, he moved his right leg. It twinged, but held nowhere near the same agonising pain as before. In fact, he could hardly feel *any* pain at all. He attempted to bend his knee just a little ... and succeeded. He bent it further, until he'd created a sharp triangle with his leg which lay on its side under the covers, his foot pushing against the inside of his left thigh.

He gulped hard, trying to calm every last nerve within, as

he watched the staff trying to resuscitate the woman; knowing they'd fail.

His knee had completely healed.

# IV
## *Pulse*

**S**he had managed to finish work at four o'clock. Not expecting to have been able to leave until well after six, she breathed a sigh of relief, delighting in the temporary lack of rain as she once again made her way across Kensington Park.

She might even be able to make it to the hospital on foot, she was so ahead of schedule.

A message had been left on her phone just ten minutes ago, telling her her 'friend' had woken up. Last night, she thought she'd have a fight on her hands asking the hospital to use her as his emergency contact considering she could claim no relation to him at all, but it turned out they were pleased to have *any* contact for him on file until the mystery of who he was could be solved. She guessed they preferred not to have sole respons-ibility for him, and it never looked good if they *didn't* have an emergency contact down for their patients.

She wasn't complaining. Perhaps it was her curious mind that had piqued and needed to solve the puzzle herself, but she was intrigued by the stranger she'd found. She also felt a sense of duty towards him she couldn't place, but she accepted it as a 'normal' reaction connected to finding him in the first place.

Her mind was distracted by a couple walking out of the Serpentine Gallery, its doors still open because it wasn't six o'clock yet.

Her footsteps ceased. She hadn't been inside in years, and she suddenly found herself with the opportunity to revisit the gallery because of her early leave from work.

Briefly, she pitted that against the need to get to the hospital as quickly as possible.

*You can spare just fifteen minutes. Mr Beautiful's not going anywhere.*

She frowned. That had to stop right now – thinking of him like *that* was a recipe for disaster. Instead, she refocused her thoughts on remembering the last time she'd come here. It had been shortly after her Madrid trip where she'd been inspired by that statue of Lucifer. In fact, if she recalled correctly, that very statue was what had her thinking she needed to visit the gallery more often, for she had stopped coming here since her parents died. It had just been too painful – they had loved this place.

Just like them, she had always loved art of any kind. Being labelled as academically clever for most of her life by admiring peers, she had always secretly felt artists were *more* clever. No matter how many chemicals she could decipher under a microscope, or how well she could read patterns in the ground or sky, she couldn't paint or draw for toffee. In her day to day life, she took handfuls of 'nothing' and was able to analyse what couldn't always be seen with the naked eye, but to be able to *create* such beautiful things out of nothing but imagination... She could only wish for such a talent. She needed the stars to already exist in order to interpret them; artists could *make* the stars.

Her feet were already taking her up the pathway towards the open doors. She felt excitement stir, even as a nostalgic sadness at the memory of her parents underlaid it.

These two weeks off was just what she needed to get back in touch with the things that mattered most; the things that made her who she was.

This building *smelt* of art.

Beautiful.

She walked in, and dropped some coins straight into the donation box standing in the entrance, and then hungrily soaked in everything surrounding her, from abstract designs of things purposely left to loose interpretation, to slick oil paintings, both modern and old, depicting stormy seas, blue skies, and a hundred things in between.

Ten minutes sped by far too quickly.

The final room in the gallery yet to explore at the break-neck pace she was setting, displayed a sign outside it advising unsuitability for children – a one week only exhibition, ending today: *La Petite Mort.*

Evie walked in, heart beating just that little bit faster, because *this* room was certainly atmospheric – decadently so – with darkened lighting; dark rose, velvet drapes across windows and ceiling beams, and a breathtaking show of phenomenal imagery depicting deviant sexuality among those in throes of death.

"Wow..." she let slip between her lips, unbidden heat creeping up her back from her coccyx at the ambience alone, much less the erotic scenes captured in the frames which surrounded her.

She was alone in this room, but a thousand eyes watched her, each painting, statue and photograph promising to come alive at her presence.

She shook her head at the crazy thought. *Art is so powerful.*

Still, the heat rose, like a living coil weaving around her spine, impregnating itself within her DNA.

Her gaze fixed on a renaissance painting of a woman on her back, hand clutching her breast; curled, golden hair spread across a pillow as she tilted her head back in what could only be ecstasy. But her eyes were glazed over, mostly white, as if in death.

Another, more modern painting showed yet another wo-man on her back, on a bed, a male's head (hooded, Grim Reaper style) between her legs as his skeletal hand grasped her hip.

*Why are all these women on their backs?*

Ignoring the obvious wetness spreading across her groin, she continued to look.

She was hard-pressed to find any man in a submissive posi-tion. There were a couple, but they weren't obvious enough. Really ... it wasn't like she was a die-hard feminist or anything, but what was wrong with a *man* submitting to ecstasy? Even in death? Why was it the woman who had to make the sacrifice? And why did pleasure have to equal sacrifice in the first place?

Her attention wandered to a large, vertical oil painting on the far wall opposite the door, and she gasped. Her favourite! She recognised it straight away because this had *always* been her favourite painting, ever since she first clapped eyes on it as a teenager: *Lilith*, by John Collier.

They'd transported it here from its usual home in South-port? Just for this exhibition?

She stepped towards it, in total awe of the mastery of the piece; every strand of that long, red, flowing hair handled with such delicacy; the scales on the serpent entwined around the length of Lilith's body, perfect to behold. The painting was even more beautiful in the flesh, so to speak, although...

She squinted at it, only a couple of feet away from the frame. Lilith's hair looked more blonde than red up close. It must be a trick of the light, because she swore, with each passing second, her hair looked blonder than before.

The sun gleamed off the scales of the snake, making her

blink.

*What?*

Glancing at the window, she could only make out darkness beyond the pane. Even if she could *see* the sun behind all that cloud cover up there, it would have mostly already set by now.

*An optical illusion.*

She looked back at the painting, and took an involuntary step back, eyes widening in shock. *The scales* ... the snake was...

*Holy shit!* She blinked again, rapidly, more than once, then looked up again. *It's not moving – don't be a dunce.*

Another step back.

Her hair was *definitely* lighter than before. In fact, it was no longer red at all. Just a shimmering golden-blonde.

*That's not Lilith...* hissed a quiet voice in her mind ... an *ancient* voice.

The heat in her sparked, and a liquid flame licked up her spine, weaving its way around her back, groin and waist, mirroring every contour of the serpent's body; firing off her nerve-endings until she broke out in goosebumps.

"The little death."

She yelped; spun on her heel, half numb, yet half in fright.

"That's what the French call an orgasm, you know – the little death."

Blood pulsed in her ears as she came back to ground. Mild irritation replaced startlement. "Mark?" she said, just about managing to sound out his name from her tight throat.

God damn it, had he *followed* her here?

He must have read the hard look in her eye correctly. He rushed ahead with, "Wait. Please wait. I wanted to apologise. I called your name before you left the museum, but you must have been preoccupied – you didn't hear me, and you walked off in such a rush. And then, I wasn't sure if it was you I saw walking in here, you were so far up ahead of me, but I thought

I'd take a chance, because..." he sighed. "I didn't mean to make a dick of myself, or make you feel pressured, or anything like that. I just wanted you to know that. I enjoy your company, that's all. There aren't a lot of people I can talk science with, or rubbish with." He smiled in an attempt to lighten the mood.

To be honest, it was working. That smile was a charmer – sweet and a little cheeky – setting off both a small dimple in his left cheek, and the lighter shade of the grey in his eyes. Add the mop of slightly dishevelled dark hair, and it's not like he was a bad looker or anything.

Guilt returned, and she suddenly felt a little embarrassed about her reaction yesterday. Hell, he hadn't really done anything at all to upset her.

*Defensive much?* chided her more familiar inner-voice. Because it was just like her to get defensive around men if they showed too much interest – Philip's wonderful legacy, and a pattern she really needed to break.

"I'd very much like us to be friends," he continued. "*Just* friends – although, I understand if you'd rather just ... not. If you'd rather play it safe. I respect what you said about not looking for a relationship."

God. What was she doing? "Mark... Last night I was cold and wet, and hungry." She gave him a small smile of her own. It was enough to make him sag his shoulders in obvious relief she wasn't blocking him out of her life. "I can get a bit defensive when... I mean, I *meant* what I said, about not looking for a relationship, and as long as that's okay with you, I'd love to be friends. I think you're great – you *have* been great. I don't want to lose that."

This was no less awkward than when he'd left her last night, but against the strange intensity of this room, she was all at once glad for the awkwardness. It was real, and tangible, and it made sense.

Art had always moved her, but it didn't always make sense – she got lost in it so easily. Still smiling at Mark, she turned her head to glance quickly behind her.

There was her beloved painting, looking very two-dimensional, and Lilith's hair was one hundred percent *red*.

*Your imagination... You're such a child, Evie.*

She let out a small sigh and turned back to Mark, whose smile was now big and bright. "Great. That's great. Well ... without any pressure, of course, I'm happy to walk you home if you'd like me to. Or not." He brought his arms up in a peaceful gesture.

Evie laughed. "Was I that bad?"

"With the force of a battalion."

"I'm sorry."

"No problem."

"I would say yes to the company, but I'm actually off to see a friend in hospital."

"Oh," his smile fell into a concerned frown. "I'm so sorry. Jesus," he shook his head, "I didn't even think as to the reason why you were rushing off."

She kept from telling him it had been more down to excitement than worry. "It's okay – I think he's out of the woods." She didn't miss the minuscule tightening of his jawline on the mention of the 'he' she let slip. But it went as quickly as it had come. Good. Her 'just friends' rule was one she was determined to keep.

"I certainly hope so." He cleared his throat. "Perhaps I can give you a call after Christmas and all the family obligations that come with it, and we can catch up over lunch, or something."

It was her turn to stiffen. He had no idea about her family, or lack of it, and it was something she never talked about. If they were going to be friends, she supposed she should tell him, but she was so private about her personal stuff, that idea didn't sit right with her just yet. "That would be nice. After Christmas."

"Okay then. I'll text you."

She nodded, and then made towards the door with him following.

"You sure you'll be fine making your way to the hospital?"

"No problem. It's not a long journey, and look," she waved at the sky from where they now stood by the front entrance. "No rain."

He chuckled. "Enjoy it while it lasts."

"Oh, I will. Have a wonderful Christmas, Mark." After a pause, she held out her hand to him.

He smiled warmly and took it.

It *was* warm, and almost ... familiar.

This actually was the most 'familiar' they'd been with each other. *See? It's not so bad. You don't have to shut everyone out.*

She couldn't help but think back to last night when her hand had grazed that man's as they'd been lying on the road. That had been like a lightning bolt to her core. She was almost convinced she'd made it up; that it had been the result of that sense of 'danger' and nothing more.

*Imagination – wild.*

"I will. You too, Evie. Merry Christmas."

"Merry Christmas."

He left before her, and she waved goodbye after him.

She got the fright of her life when she peeked at her watch and noticed it had gone five o'clock. No *way* had she been in there a whole hour!

But of course she had. That's just what happened when she looked at statues and paintings – she drifted off and lost herself, just like in Madrid. "Great," she muttered.

Without wasting another second, she strode out of the gallery and headed towards the north gate of the park, debating whether she should walk to St Mary's Hospital, or take the bus.

She decided on the bus so she wouldn't miss visiting hours, and then she'd still have time to eat dinner, even if she decided to walk home from St Mary's.

Good. She had a plan.

*Let's just hope the plan listens.*

~*~

He had no plan.

Just hunger pangs, utter confusion, and a near empty box of tissues.

No one had been back to check on him in over an hour, and what exactly he was going to say when he was asked about his miraculous recovery, he didn't know. So far, he was going with nothing. It's not like he had an answer that made sense, although he did have a very weird one he wasn't going to tell anyone, ever.

His stomach growled.

*What do I have to do to get some food around here?*

He wanted to get up and stretch his legs, but he didn't want to face the explanation he wouldn't be able to give when he got caught walking around like he was doing just fine.

Best to postpone the awkward inevitable for as long as possible. Or at least until he could figure out who the fuck he was, should his brain cells choose to comply.

Shadows crept into the edge of his vision to his right.

He turned and found himself looking at the unconscious man next to him once more. The effect of his medication was waning, causing...

*Good god, not again!*

It wasn't *quite* the same. That familiar ache drove deep into his navel, making his ever perverse penis tingle, but the sensation was less lustful, and driven more by a need he didn't understand.

Not that he'd understood his earlier need either.

This man wasn't dying. It wasn't death he was attracted to this time but the shadows that flitted around the patient, projected by his own soul. He could *clearly* see them.

*Demons...* whispered his mind. *They're his demons.*

Well, wasn't that just fucking wonderful.

As the ache in him took over the hunger pangs, he wondered if it would be better if he *never* got his memory back. Whoever he was, he was clearly deranged. He could do with *not* going back to that.

*There's no escaping it, you piece of shit – even if you remember nothing, this will follow you. You'll still need to deal with THIS.*

He inwardly groaned in despair and shut his eyes, but the shadows still licked the corners of them, not leaving him be, and beckoning him like a moth to a sea of dark flames.

He opened them again; stared at the man.

He wanted him to wake. He wanted him to face his 'demons' so he could see him fighting them; see them strip him of everything he held onto.

*The only way to truth.*

His head was fucked up. Maybe he *hadn't* been this way at all, and whatever accident had landed him in here had made him like this.

In an attempt to disengage from whatever the hell was taking over his being, he looked at the other patients in the room, some awake, some asleep, but... *Oh, fuck.*

Heated tears of both anger and fear surfaced, right along with that same disgust he'd felt earlier at his burning centre.

They *all* had shadows.

*Demons,* corrected his mind.

*Shut up!* he shouted back.

He didn't want to, but he zeroed in on a woman – young – lying on the far left corner of the room in the darkest part of the ward. She was awake – he could make out that she was blinking – but she was black and blue, her face swollen and covered in bruises; a brace around her neck; the scent of violence and tears swimming in the air around her.

The story of what had happened to her played out for him to see, just like it had with the woman, earlier, who had died. However, this lady was nowhere near death either.

But her vulnerability … *Jesus.*

There.

That fire shooting up his cock, causing it to harden.

He growled, and shoved his hand over his crotch, scrunching the bedsheets as he fought to hold the damn thing down. *No!*

The heady concoction of her shame and vulnerability was like an elixir he could taste, and *by god*, if she let it – if she *let* it – it would make her invincible. But first she needed to cry, to scream, to feel the torture of acceptance for what had taken place, for her violation, and he wanted to help her with that.

He gripped his sheets tighter as the twisted urge dominated his abdomen.

He could help her with it all; aid her rise into grace like a phoenix reborn—

"Hi."

He all but jumped in his bed at the softest of voices; turned; froze.

What a vision.

And it wasn't just the long, blonde hair that surrounded her like a crown of untainted immaculacy, or her big, blue eyes that seemed to see him for exactly what he was. Although that couldn't be the case, for surely she would run screaming.

It was the fact that she held no shadows.

He blinked at her, astounded; brought his left leg up at the knee – his good knee – to hide his monstrous erection.

No. She had no shadows at all. No trace of any demon, as if she'd been made with all the dark bits taken out.

*You're thinking nonsense.*

Nevertheless, she was... *Pure*, was the word his mind conjured.

And she was his.

*Not yours.*

And all of a sudden, he was split in two, half of him fighting with the other ... *mine, not mine, mine, not mine...*

"Hi," he managed to form on his tongue, for some reason afraid she would disappear if he moved or uttered a sound.

She did the opposite. On hearing his greeting, she smiled a smile he was suddenly certain he would die for in a second without any regret. It lit up the room; it lit up her; it lit up *him* from the darkest part of his being, and won his internal argument.

*Mine.*

# V
## *Returned*

**S**he half wished she'd never spoken. In fact, the minute she'd seen him from the doorway, she'd almost turned and walked the other way – he looked so ... haunted.

The staff had filled her in on his amnesia. It's not as if he would even remember who she was, so it would be no loss to him if she just disappeared.

But, like a magnet pulled towards him, she couldn't turn away.

And she'd made him a promise. She hated breaking promises, which is why she almost never made them. At least until he got his memory back, it was one she intended to keep.

Then, still unaware of her presence, he had suddenly groaned and gripped his abdomen as if in pain. It had knocked her out of her daydream state, standing there by the door.

She had made her way to him, silently, afraid of ... she didn't know what, exactly.

"Hi," she'd mumbled, frustrated she couldn't voice the single word more confidently.

He'd startled.

*Shit.*

And then, he'd turned, and some part of her had fallen, like when in an elevator, descending, and your stomach takes a second to catch up with the rest of you.

'Haunted' was the understatement of the last hundred years.

And here they were.

*Say something else. Reassure him.*

Nothing came out. She stood there and bloody gawped at him like a goldfish, an apology on the tip of her tongue, except she all at once felt that 'sorry' was not enough. As if she needed to apologise for a lifetime of brutality.

*Stupid...* it had been like that with Philip – she had *always* felt responsible for all his ails, even though she'd been the cause of none of them.

"Hi," came the reply, tight and... *Oh* ... so pained.

But it was relief she felt at his greeting. She smiled as it fell over her, inexplicably grateful for his response, as if some long-awaited key had just found a lock.

Her inner-self laughed at her. *You should have been a writer of lyrics and songs, you scientist, you...*

*I just want him to be okay,* she reasoned. The way she'd found him ... that was all it was – the need for him to make it.

"Do I ... know you?"

Her eyes widened at his question as she chided herself for her immensely poor communication skills. "No ... well, I mean, yes, sort of. I, um ... I was the one who found you. On my street. Outside my house."

He continued to drill into her with those black, black orbs.

She suppressed a shiver, unable to decipher the exact cause of it. It had her taking one step closer to him, though. "But you didn't know me before then. That was the first time I'd ever seen you." *I think*, she added silently to herself, remembering the way he'd said her name as he'd held her face so tightly.

Another shiver. Unrepressed this time.

"You're cold," he said suddenly, his gaze now on her frame.

That wasn't why she was shivering. "I'm always a little cold," was what came out instead – not a lie. Even with the heaters on, her hands and feet seemed always on the verge of frostbite.

His eyes met hers again, and she almost reeled back from the absolute understanding she saw in them now. "Me, too."

She took a last step closer, causing the zip of her coat to sound a little 'clang' as it met the metal frame of his bed.

"I'm sorry," he said, "I ... er ... I don't remember you."

"Oh, I know – it's okay. I spoke briefly to the doctors when I got here. They filled me in. They said they were going to come by and check on you in an hour or so, after dinner."

"Dinner?" he asked, surprised.

She smiled again, unable to help it. There was something almost childlike about his expression. Had no one ever fed him before? "Yes, it's on the way. I saw them doing the rounds down the corridor. They have this duty here where they have to keep you alive."

Clearly not expecting her gentle teasing, the very depth of his eyes seemed to light up, his entire face taking on a devilishly mischievous tone – as if he was going to eat her right up for that comment, and make her enjoy it – but it was gone in less than a second.

Her involuntary response to that look was anything but gone, still pounding throughout her body with every beat of her heart.

What *was* it about him? All her senses were tingling and they'd only exchanged a few sentences. He set her alight with his presence, and she'd like to think she wasn't so shallow that it was all to do with how he looked. Without a doubt, he was beautiful and *sculpted* to perfection ... lord! But there was something else. She couldn't place it. But she knew she had to nip it in the bud.

Immediately.

She had no idea who he was. *He* had no idea who he was.

He could have a family – a wife and kids. Her gaze settled on his ring finger, already knowing he'd had no jewellery, or even a watch on his person when she'd found him, but... *No tan line.*

She tore her eyes away from him, forcing her stare onto the machines next to him, trying to look like she knew what the hell they were telling her with their numbers and lines. "Have they mentioned when you're likely to come out?"

A pause.

This man seemed to consider everything before he spoke, as if he worried every question might be a trick. But then, that made sense if he had no memory of anything. How awful. How could one know what was real and what wasn't? "No. I haven't seen anyone since I woke up – a couple of hours ago, I think. I guess I might find out after dinner."

"Good. And you *look* good."

His eyebrows went up.

*Fuck!* NOT what she meant! "I mean, you look well ... as in better. Than you did when I found you." Yeah ... her cheeks were burning. She hoped the horrible fluorescent ceiling lights dulled the red down to nothing.

*He can see right through you,* teased the voice in her head, and wasn't that the truth. His dark stare penetrated her like he had bloody x-ray vision.

Slowly – ever so slowly – his lips curved upwards.

She all but died. Seriously. She swore her heart actually slowed down to a stop, her entire existence now resting on the way the corner of his lips snaked into a smile that would be the end of her. It would blind her out of sense.

Abruptly, she stepped back.

The smile stopped just as quickly, froze into place, and then fell.

There was that guilt again, spearing her. *Damn ... smile*

*again.* And she wished it with the strength of a thousand suns, even if it meant her ruination.

He didn't smile, but looked away.

Embedded in that moment, something in her changed. She felt the 'click' it made as this new thing settled, forming a dangerous clarity, and it came wrapped in every warning a mother gives her daughter; that best friends give each other; that women passed down to women. Warning against a single, reoccurring, debilitating thought that spanned generations: *My ruination is better than his.*

"I don't remember what I look like."

Snapping out of her daze—*what the hell WAS that*—she dove into her handbag, fumbling. "I have ... er ... a mirror in here ... somewhere." Bingo. She brought out the small rectangular object. "It's tiny, I'm afraid, but here you go." She held it out to him.

A faint look of trepidation crossed his features. She lowered her hand, not wanting to be the cause of his discomfort, but he leaned over, fast as lightning, and clasped the mirror from her.

Her fingers brushed his, but she'd already bitten her lip in anticipation of the gasp she didn't want him to hear. *Good. You need to control your crazy reactions. He's just a man for fuck's sake. What in god's name is wrong with you?*

Despite her very sensible talking to, a jolt of electricity passed from him to her – or maybe it was from her to him – just like it had last night.

She grabbed one of the rubber bumpers encircling the metal bed rail to ground her energy.

He met her eyes. Seemed to like doing that. A lot. "Thank you," he said.

Had he felt that jolt, or had it been just her? He uttered not a word about it.

*Hello, Miss Selfish – why should he? You're hardly on his list of priorities. He has a hundred other things to worry about.*

Sitting back against his pillow, he opened the compact mirror and looked at himself.

She jumped when he exhaled, sharply; anger and fear taking over all else. He slammed the lid shut and shoved the thing back at her, head turned the other way.

Shocked, she took it, longing to understand what had just happened; what he'd seen; what to say to make everything better.

"It's okay if you leave."

Wounded breath escaped her.

"You don't have to stay."

Stupidly, tears filled her eyes at his rejection of her.

*What. Just. Happened?*

Before she could find words, a trolley of food was wheeled in; two bubbly nurses filling the distraught silence. "Good evening, Mr Lucky," one of them giggled, but with no malice.

Evie threw her a glare she didn't notice. *Mr what?*

*Get a grip!* She was losing it, and she didn't even know why. Blinking back the nonsensical tears, she turned and walked out, not knowing what else to do, every step weighted with regret; every inch that took her away from him, coated in a stifled scream that demanded she go back.

Strangely numb, and very confused, she walked out the doorway of the ward, turned left, and let her back fall against the wall, unable to shake the feeling she'd just failed some unknown mission.

*Why are you always trying to help people who don't want to be helped?*

She didn't know him, she had no hold on him; had no business being in his life at all.

What was she supposed to do now?

With a sigh, still trying to shake off the sense she was somehow doing something wrong, she lifted herself off the wall and looked around for the way out.

*Call it quits, Evie. Time to go home.*

~*~

*She didn't see ... she didn't see ... she didn't see...*

She hadn't seen, had she?

He shook as a plate loudly hit his tray. Everything sounded too loud – even the rustle of sheets as the nurses made his bedding more comfortable.

He hoped they were too focused on their task to notice the shaking.

Clasping his hands together, he forced himself still ... tried.

His hands looked fine. Not at all like what he'd seen in the... Not like his face.

*See? It's you. You're imagining it, like you've imagined everything else.*

But why in the hell would he imagine *that*?

*Why have you imagined everything you've imagined from the moment you woke up?*

"Okay, Mr Lucky..."

Did they *have* to call him that?

"...we'll leave you in peace to eat. Doctors will be by soon, all right?"

He nodded, not trusting his voice.

*She didn't see, she didn't see, she didn't see...*

And neither did the nurses. They couldn't see, or they'd be running a mile; locking him up.

*Or cutting you open.*

Eat.

That's all he had to do. Eat and hold it the fuck together.

He wished he hadn't told the blonde woman to leave – his only friend.

*No one's your friend. You have no friends.*

He fixed his eyes on the food. It looked shit, but it was a damn sight better than...

Bile rose in his throat, bringing tears that stung his eyes.

What he'd seen – that wasn't him.

*It's more you than this. You think* this *is you? This body with arms and legs? Not even close.*

The nurses left.

Thank fuck.

He grabbed the fork from the tray now in front of him, but couldn't hold it still, he was trembling so much.

*Monster.*

It was hard to breathe.

His face... He'd looked like...

Desperately, he shoved his fork right in his mouth with whatever food he'd managed to get on it. He missed, and pricked his lip with one of the prongs.

*You degenerate.*

Wincing at the sharp pain, he instinctively licked his lip of the blood. A bolt of euphoria shot through him at the sharp tang of it, unmistakeable and impossible to shut out. It tore a path straight to his loins.

He gripped his fork so hard he bent it; gritted his teeth – *Noooo, not again, not again, not again.*

A shadow fell over him from his left, and he jerked in his bed, ready to defend himself by whatever means possible.

"It's me."

Her hand fell on his arm without hesitation, her soothing warmth as instantaneous as the invasion of his body a second ago – a body he seemed unable to control.

It calmed under her touch, and he stared at her in nothing less than shock. If he'd hurt her feelings, she showed no sign of it. She emanated only kindness, and a faint layer of sadness he connected with, which nestled in the depths of her blue eyes.

"I was going to leave," she said, softly, "but I made you a promise, you see – when I found you – that I wouldn't leave you. And even if you don't remember it, I always keep my promises."

She'd come back – this stranger.

He stared at her, wide-eyed. *She came back.*

Hand still on his arm, she placed her other over the one clenched around his fork, his knuckles white from his death-grip.

It was as if he melted under her, all cold fading away.

The fork slipped from his grasp. He broke.

Tucking his chin under, tears streaked and he heaved out sobs he could no longer contain under the weight of confusion, loneliness, and some dark seed of terror he couldn't quench.

Her warmth continued to envelop him, none spared, as she gently brought him towards her and rested her head on his.

*She came back.*

Her hand on his arm travelled along his back until he was held in her embrace.

"Th-Thank you," he spluttered out, his words of gratitude as messy as the rest of him.

"You're welcome."

# VI
## *Push*

Evie didn't know if this was the kind of thing her parents would have had a fit over, or praised her for, but standing there at the reception desk, waiting to take him home while papers were filled out, it felt right. It felt good. It felt better than squeezing him into the last bed at the YMCA two days before Christmas, when she had a spare bedroom at hers.

His physical recovery had been nothing short of miraculous. It had the doctors scratching their heads and comparing x-ray results and MRI scans. His mental recovery though, was still stuck at first base. He had no idea who he was, where he'd come from, or whether he had any relatives in the area. He didn't really even seem to know the area.

Missing persons reports, via the police – even MIA British Army lists – had thrown up nothing to solve the mystery. And it's not like he could be mistaken from description. He was six foot two for starters. No one they had searched through fit his attributes exactly.

He looked up at the nurse from his papers. Her name badge read **Nurse S. Rankin**. "I don't know how to sign this," he said.

She smiled. "Just sign it 'Mr Lucky'. You have witnesses and *we* all know who you are."

Yes. He was quite famous among staff at the hospital now.

He frowned slightly, and filled the signature line with his temporary name, concentrating so hard on the letters, Evie's heart went out to him. She wondered if his own writing was alien to him. Probably. Still, at least he knew how to write and read. It seemed the only elements of life he couldn't remember were directly related to himself. There was a name for that kind of amnesia, according to the doctors, but she couldn't remember what it was off the top of her head. Weekly appointments had been arranged for him at the hospital with a clinical psychologist.

"There." He seemed to sigh with relief as he put the pen down.

The nurse thanked him and handed the pen to Evie. She'd already been briefed on all of this over the past couple of days. She signed on the line as one of his witnesses, and also the other two sections that confirmed her responsibility for the patient at her address.

A nurse and a doctor, finalised everything with their own signatures, and that was it. "Okay, we're done," grinned the nurse. "Have a wonderful Christmas, Mr Lucky."

Evie held back a laugh as he cringed at his given 'name'. "Well, they have to call you *something*," she'd reasoned with him, yesterday.

"Does it have to be the name one gives to a dog?" he'd retorted.

Under all that vulnerability, he had a very dry, steely sense of humour Evie was starting to catch glimpses of bit by bit. She liked it. "Come on," she said to him now as she popped her bag over her shoulder.

He hesitated. "You're still sure?"

She rolled her eyes to the heavens. "For the thousandth time, yes."

He gulped, clearly grateful, but ever on edge. "You know I

could be—"

"Dangerous. A psychopath. A serial killer. Got it."

He frowned again.

"You might also be a loving husband and father whose family would be grateful for the room I'm offering. I know if I had a husband, I would be. I wouldn't want him in a homeless shelter, especially not at Christmas. Not when I have the space, and the bed at the shelter could be given to someone else who *actually* needs it. We've been through this, and my mind hasn't changed."

Turmoil crossed his countenance. This man didn't do anything by halves. Thankfully, the internal agony faded from his features and he finally took a step towards her with a small smile. "I don't know how to thank you."

"I like my feet massaged."

He stalled, surprised.

She laughed. "I'm kidding. Well ... I *do* like my feet massaged, but you're relieved of the task. There's no thanks needed. Seeing you fully recovered will be thanks enough."

After what felt like almost five minutes, they stood at the entrance of the hospital. The clouds looked heavy, but the crazy torrential shower that had come down an hour ago had stopped. With any luck, it would hold off. "Bus or walk?"

"Oh..." He looked around, completely lost. "Walk? Maybe it'll help if I ... I don't know. See some sights or something. Get a feel for the area."

"Good idea. This way. It's about half an hour's walk from mine. Sound okay?"

"After almost a week sitting or lying down, it sounds like bliss."

"Great."

They fell into an easy silence, occasionally filled with conversation starters and small talk. She didn't mind. Living on her own for so long, silence was something she was used to, and this man's silences were so full of his intensity it didn't feel like silence at all. "So ... what are we going to do about your name?" she asked.

He glanced at her quizzically. "I beg your pardon?"

"If you don't want me to buy you a lead and some chew toys, perhaps we should change it?"

The set of his jaw answered her question for her. Stifling another laugh, she kicked a stone as they crossed a road, all the streets across London so much emptier since all the craziness ten years ago. "Do you have any idea at all what it could be?"

"My name? No."

"Is there a name you like? That you're drawn to?"

"No. Perhaps whoever or whatever hit my head also knocked my imagination out of me."

*Oh* ... he was *so* damn dry. It was intriguing. It was like a challenge – to reach his softness; get him smiling.

*No, no! Not going there, remember? Men don't need fixing. What is that? That's the woman you never wanted to be, remember? Women don't 'fix' men. That crap belongs only in romance novels. Reality check!*

She clenched her teeth at her scolding self. "We should keep it simple," she stated, Kensington Park now in sight. "Let's work with what you've already got."

"And what's that?"

"Lucky," she smiled.

He scowled.

She grinned. "Luck."

"I've got luck?"

"Certainly do. We shouldn't take that away. Maybe just shorten it a bit more."

"I still don't—"

"Luc."

He stopped walking, bringing her to a halt also.

"L U C," she explained. "Lucky, shortened."

"Luc?"

"Luc."

He stared at her for an eternity. She had to look down. "Unless, of course, you hate it, in which case—"

"It's perfect."

She looked back up, surprised at his earnest. "It is?"

"Yes." He shook his head slightly. "Your mind is like a whirlwind."

She shoved him playfully in the side with her shoulder. "Good job too, since yours is empty."

She wasn't expecting his laugh, not having once heard him laugh in the past week. It was a rich thing, both deep and piercing at the same time. And for the millionth time she wondered what the hell she was doing. Here. With him. Because she couldn't deny her attraction, yet she had to for both of them. He needed his memory back, and she needed to pre-empt a swift goodbye when that happened because no way in hell was this guy single. She could paint it any way she wanted – that she was doing the right thing morally; being the good Samaritan – but the truth was, she liked him, and she wanted time to get to know him better before he disappeared.

She chewed on her lip, wondering whether to tell him the truth from the start. Crap. That felt like placing a burden on him, though. He didn't need that from her. And he might just run if he knew.

*Damn.* Why did the thought of him running eat her up? She hadn't cared an iota that all the men – not that there had been many – in her life had disappeared eventually. But with him – *Luc* – it mattered. As if his disappearance would end her somehow. *You're in so much fucking trouble. You should never have brought him back.*

"Earth to Eve."

"Huh? Oh ... it's Evie."

"Sorry."

"No, I'm sorry. Didn't mean to drift off."

They entered the park.

"Is Evie short for something?"

"Evelyn. Everyone calls me Evie. Only my parents ever called me Eve – or Evelyn if I did something wrong."

She felt, rather than saw, his stare on her. "What?"

"You used past tense when referring to your parents."

*Astute.* "They died."

"Shit. I'm so—"

"It's fine, it was ten years ago now."

"How—"

"Plane crash."

"That's ... harsh."

She shrugged. "I don't think there's a non-harsh way to lose your parents." She breathed out, unsure as to why she was about to divulge the next piece of information. "They were my adopted parents. I mean, they adopted me, when I was around two or three. I don't remember it. I don't remember anything before them, so as far as I was concerned, they were my real parents. They were good people – always honest with me. Always made sure I knew the truth about my background, and were always supportive with it, and of whatever decision I made."

"Wow."

"Yeah. Maybe it's rare – to have parents like that. I hope not," she laughed. "Anyway, my name was always Evelyn – that's what they told me. It's on my birth certificate, but with no surname."

"No surname?"

"Nope. Just Evelyn. I don't know how my birth-mum got

away with it, but there you go. I can only hazard a guess as to why she didn't want to use her own surname. Nothing like a mother who doesn't want you to find her."

"There could be many reasons," he said, quietly.

*Yeah, right.*

"Does it grate you?"

"That she didn't want me to find her? Maybe a little. It never used to, but since my parents died ... you just begin to wonder, you know? You just think about different options."

Silence ensued as they passed the Serpentine Gallery.

"We have something in common, then," Luc finally piped up. "We both have no names – in a sense. I have none at all, and you have no surname."

Evie smiled. "I took on my adopted parents' surname: Gold."

"Evie Gold. I like it. It suits you."

She blushed at the compliment, half-perturbed that he got her blood rising so easily. "Thank you. I've always thought so, too. Maybe we need to pick a surname for you as well."

"What's the opposite of gold?"

"What?" she asked, bemused.

"What's the opposite of gold?" he repeated, seemingly not aware of how strange his question was.

"Er ... silver?"

"No – that's similar to gold."

"Then, I don't know," she laughed again, feeling a little uncomfortable, although she couldn't fathom why.

"How about 'dark'?" he continued. "What about 'black'?"

"Um—"

"Gold is bright and shiny and luminescent, just like you. I feel very much the opposite of you—"

"That's daft—"

"Lost; no memory; there's just this shadow where—"

She grabbed his arm and brought him to a stop. "So you want to be called Luc Black?" He'd hit a button she didn't know was there. "You'd pick a name that symbolises everything you *don't* want to be? Everything you're trying to overcome?"

His expression all at once became guarded, giving nothing away, and it only pissed her off more that 'Black' suited his demeanour down to the ground, because something inside told her it shouldn't. When had this silly little name game turned so serious?

He couldn't or wouldn't answer her.

"Luc means 'light'," she pressed. "Did you know that? So your choice of surname makes no sense."

"And what does Evelyn mean?" he shot back at her.

Another blush rose, but she raised her head with it, not willing to let him win at his debilitating way of thinking. "Life."

Their eyes locked.

*Nope – not gonna win.*

"Life." God ... *his voice.* 'Intense' was an *understatement* for this man. He might as well have given birth to the word on his hushed tone.

His stare bored into hers.

Prickles danced across her skin.

"The first breath," he added, barely at a whisper.

Time seemed to stand still.

A heavy, fat drop of rain hit her shoulder, breaking the odd atmosphere between them. They both looked up.

"Quick," she tugged on his arm. "It'll cascade without warning. I'm just five minutes away."

Their bizarre conversation ended right there.

~*~

He shouldn't be here, for as much as he didn't know about himself, he *did* know things he hadn't told her – dark, awful things about the way he thought; the way he reacted. *Not normal.* But he was selfish.

*Selfish, selfish.*

He was drawn to this woman like she was his life-saving beacon. Not that she'd denied that role one bit – had insisted on it, in fact.

Still ... he should have pushed her away, but he had been weak, and still was. Weak of mind; weak of heart. "Your home is beautiful," he said.

She smiled as she shut the front door behind them. "Thank you. Consider it yours for a short while."

"Ours," he corrected. Then felt shitty for saying it. He had no right to impose on her life like this.

She didn't seem to take any offence, but began to strip off her outer clothing.

He did the same with the coat and shoes she had bought for him – another thing he would need to repay her for. "I hate that I'm dripping water onto your floor."

She waved off his concern. "It's wooden – it'll wipe clean. Here." She handed him a towel she'd picked up from the coat stand. "Every day I bring the rain in, so I keep this to hand."

He took it from her and ran it over his hair and neck. "It rains every day?"

She glanced at him with interest. "You don't remember that? The quakes ten years ago?"

Half-used to the sense of abandonment each time his memory evaded him, he shook his head.

"It was the closest thing to Armageddon this world has experienced."

"I doubt that."

She stared at him a beat, quizzically, and he returned the

look. He didn't really know where that statement of his had come from.

"I thought it was only the things about yourself you couldn't remember."

He attempted a smile. "Perhaps I had something to do with Armageddon."

The poor joke fell flat in her dark hallway, his tone sounding sinister even though he'd tried to make it light.

*Note to self: you suck at people skills.*

She let out a small laugh. He couldn't tell whether it was at his awkwardness, or to cut the thick air he'd inadvertently created.

She took the towel and his coat from him and hung them both up. "I'll show you up to your room. There are a very small amount of my dad's clothes I never had the heart to give away." She wrinkled her nose. "They might be a size too small, and a bit 1990s, but they should do until we can make a proper trip to the shops. I took them out of storage a couple of days ago and gave them a wash."

"I'm sure they'll be fine, thank you."

He surveyed the house as he followed her down the hallway and towards the stairs. It was an Edwardian delight – all white walls and dark woods and oaks – but loneliness clung to every molecule like a blanket time had glued on. "Have you lived alone since your parents passed away?"

"Yes."

That was all she said, and he didn't pry further. The house felt like a time capsule – some portal to her secret self – and he was trying to figure out why, because all the décor was quite modern. Vases, paintings – *lots* of paintings – ornaments, and most things lying around were from this century as far as he could make out. A couple of magazines left on display were from the last week. "I see you like your paintings."

Her face lit up. God, he actually felt lighter for it.

"I *love* art. It makes me feel so alive."

*Maybe you're my art, then.* He kept that inappropriate thought to himself as he was led down the upstairs corridor and into the spare room.

"This used to be my room when I was younger. I sleep in what was my parents' room now. It's big and comfy in here." She looked at him expectantly, as if needing his approval.

"It's wonderful. I have no idea how to tha—"

"No more thank-yous, okay? I'm sure you'd do the same for me. Let's just concentrate on getting your memories back."

He nodded and walked towards the window.

He felt her come up behind him, her faint breath on his shoulder. He fought the urge to turn and take her into his arms. *Shouldn't have come here...*

He was a first class pleb for avoiding the fact he was attracted to her and had been since he'd first seen her at the hospital. He'd convinced himself he could handle it; that the attraction was just an extension of his over-reactive self, only nicer because she heralded no demons or weird death-related erections. Like a complete wuss, he felt safe with her, and he'd let that sense of safety overtake all other sense. He was pretty sure she was his best bet at getting his memories back, and that had taken precedence over anything else. *Selfish, selfish...*

"That's where I found you," she said softly, pointing out the window to where it faced, out front.

His eyes landed on the grate beside the pavement, across the road. "It's so quiet. It's the weekend. Where are all the people? The cars?"

She shook her head, sadly. "I hardly see anyone anymore. A lot of people moved out of the city after the quakes. London's not how it used to be. Even when I travel to Oxford for work twice a week, it's like a ghost town – everywhere's like that."

"It seems strange."

"It is, but I've kind of gotten used to it."

He spun around to face her.

Her eyes widened in surprise, but she didn't move. She was standing so close to him, he could feel the heat of her body.

"You're lonely," he stated. "That's not something you ever get used to."

He regretted his candidness as soon as the words were out of his mouth. Tears rose to her eyes, casting a sheen across them. So ... she had one demon after all. He reached for her, "Eve..."

"Evie," she bit out, quietly, taking a step back.

*Fuck.* "I'm sorry. That was so out of—"

"Come see the rest of the house," she cut in, and then turned and walked out of the room.

~*~

*What did you expect?*

From the second she'd laid eyes on him, she'd felt like he could see into her very soul, so that last comment of his should have come as no surprise. But it still speared her, because it was true. Was she that transparent? Or was he just the kind of guy who always knew which button to push – *even* with no memory.

*And you're pissed because he's right ... because that's why you invited him back to yours – insisted on it.*

She was lonely.

A decade of end-of-the-world insanity did that to you. She'd never thought it would be like this. She'd thought if anything catastrophic occurred on a worldwide scale, people would pull together, help each other, and, in fact, they did seem to help each other, but no one helped her ... everyone had just retreated from her; left her. *After everything you've done for them...*

Quickly, she wiped at her eyes before the tears could fall, confused as to where that self-pitying thought had come from. She'd done nothing special. She was just one insignificant person amongst hordes of others, and the world didn't owe anyone anything – her parents had taught her that. " *You make your own way, your own luck. Give what you can, when you can, and treasure any gift that comes your way as deserved.*" That had been their lesson and she believed it wholeheartedly.

Her emotions had been kind of skewed ever since Luc had entered the equation. Damn it, he was right. Having him here, in her house... It *did* enlarge the loneliness that lived within her because it had been so long since she'd had anyone here at all. But that's all it was. It was nothing she couldn't handle.

She pulled herself together as her parents' words of advice echoed through her mind. Her life was good, despite the aloneness. She *did* treasure it. This was just a blip, that was all – what goes around, comes around. She just needed to wait for the wheel to turn. "This is the bathroom on the right," she continued as they walked past it. "Also quite roomy and there's a shower, too. And here's my room on the left." *Next to yours.*

She felt the warmth creep into her face again as an unexpected self-consciousness presented itself at the thought of him standing right there, seeing her room. So stupid. It was just her goddamned bedroom. It wasn't as if she was on the bed, naked, and spread-eagled in front of him.

*Oh, fuck,* she frowned, looking away, face going redder. *Great imagery, Evie. Get that one out of your mind.*

She cleared her throat. "Don't ... um..." *Don't say it.* "Don't feel you can't come in here, or anything." *Oh, Evie,* her head laughed at her. *Nothing says 'desperate for it' more than an invitation into your bedroom. Especially when that invite is given to a complete stranger.* "I mean, if you need anything." *Making it worse.* "No ... I mean, you know, in the night, or something." *Oh, GOD.*

Her breath quietly whooshed out of her. She couldn't take any air back in. With utter trepidation at her vocal clumsiness, and an apology screaming from her mind, she looked at Luc, only to find him grinning from ear to ear.

It didn't help her struggle for air, because if this man was beautiful looking glum, he was positively stunning when happy. But it did stir a slither of indignation. *Cheeky bastard.* "So ... it's one of those days when everything I'm saying is coming out wrong."

The grin didn't diminish. "I know the feeling well. In fact, I may have created it."

How completely odd that his flippant comment at her embarrassing verbal clumsiness sounded like one of the most sincere things she'd ever heard from anyone.

She suddenly realised that was one of the reasons she liked him – Luc led to craziness. Everything about him seemed unexpected and back-to-front – chaotic – and she loved it. It made her feel ... whole. As if his 'wrongness' made her rightness *better* somehow.

She found herself grinning back at him through her humiliation. "Tea?"

"That British solution to all things awkward? I'd love a cup, thank you."

Just like that, genuine, impulsive laughter – hers and his – filled her house for the first time in a long time. She led him out of the room and back down the stairs. Through his easy acceptance of it, her embarrassment faded almost as quickly as it had risen, and they both relaxed into the rest of the afternoon.

# VII
## *Fall*

*H*e watched from the shadows as the kid was beaten up. Six on one – hardly fair, but that was life.

As the hidden voyeur, his entire body thrummed from the ripples of energy coming off the kid in waves and reaching him where he stood; ripples that vibrated with every hit the boy took; with every cry that was wrenched from his lungs.

He was only seventeen.

The boy's life story played out before his eyes, as everyone's did when they were teetering on the edge of this world.

Normally, he didn't take any pleasure from witnessing the destructive tendencies of the younger ones. Sure – their fall was always explosive; magnificent. The young ones had tons upon tons of energy to spare, and when they loathed the world, or themselves, they loathed with a passion often lacking in adults. That pure strength of youth kept them hanging on, though, and never had them falling far enough for his needs.

But this kid was near the end. He'd almost given up, his veins coated with nine months worth of heroin, coke and got knew what else, because his entire existence made no sense without a push into the Otherworld ... to the point where the Otherworld was beginning to feel like home.

Poor blighter.

*The boy had started off certain of himself and what he wanted. He had known who he was, but somewhere along the way had lost that clarity – perhaps the same time he had lost his young male lover.*

"Fucking faggot!" shrieked one of the hooded males, older; a near-soulless gimp of societal's precious upkeep.

*He snorted to himself. Abaddon could have that one.*

*As ever, he was torn, half of him longing to help the lad under fists, and half of him knowing he would never be able to help him fully until he was dangling from that very last thread. That's when all focus became pure; when all decisions were made with a sharp truth rarely reachable in any other circumstance.*

*And on a very selfish level,* he *needed the boy's abasement; needed to feel his shame and disgrace because it quietened his own demon. Nourished it in a way no other food could accomplish, and kept him sane.*

Help will come soon, boy, *he silently consoled, knowing he wouldn't hear him. Perhaps he was consoling himself.* It just won't be in the way you think.

"Hold him down."

*A pitiful whimper, followed by pleas left the boy's lips as his jeans were torn down. He was openly sobbing now, every one of those sobs falling on deaf ears.*

*Except his, of course. There was nothing wrong with his own hearing, but like the cameraman capturing the lion hunt its prey, he did not intervene. He had a role to play.*

"No, no, no..." *came the mangled cries.*

*He ran his tongue along his teeth, pricked it on his left canine so he could taste his own blood.*

"People like you need to learn being a fudge-fucker's not a nice thing. We're your teachers, you queer little shit."

*Six on one.*

All the familiar feelings ran through him as he watched – rage, disgust, pride – as the victim's heart pulsed strongly; something all victims he'd witnessed throughout his immortal life span had in common despite the horrific events that always took place. Humans were made of strong stuff.

And then, there was his ever-present lust.

He ignored the raging tightening around his crotch – not at the despicable act unfolding before him, but at the young man's proverbial skinning – instead digging his nails into the fruit he held behind his back. Not even he could control everything.

He took it all in; absorbed every last drop of the young male's subjugation – his feelings of defeat – all the while hoping his consumption of the kid's degradation, no matter how self-serving, would unburden the boy of his pain, at least a little.

Even though he knew it never did.

He watched until his cries of 'no' became silent. He watched until the six left him, bloody, broken, and too numb to weep any more tears.

With a sideways glance at the retreating gang – pond scum on legs – he suddenly envied Abaddon's work. At least the one all beings recognised as Satan got to administer some kind of retribution; got to press the button on revenge.

He, however, got no such peace. Justice was never a luxury he was afforded to feel.

Shaking off the debilitating emotion – envy really was a crippling sin – he took a breath and emerged from his hiding place.

The kid was motionless except for his struggling to breathe, and he knew he didn't want to breathe anymore.

The last thread.

There it was.

*When he reached him, he knelt down beside him and stayed there, unmoving, until the boy's eyelids flickered through his puffy bruises and his glazed orbs found his.*

*He spread his wings, upwards and outwards, making sure it was the luminescent gold of the underside the boy saw, and not the deep red that lay on the top – that would scare him. Or maybe he was finally beyond fear.*

*The boy didn't flinch. He'd reached the end and he knew it.*

*He was right – this was the end.*

*And when standing at the very end, all else stripped away, there was only one thing left to do.*

*Wings reaching their height, he smiled at the human, his empathy on the verge of drowning him, but he'd learnt how to freeze empathy a long time ago. Good job, or he'd go under every time. "It's all right, boy. Everything's fine now." He brought the apple out from behind his back, juice leaking from where his nails had pierced its skin. He placed it against the boy's lips. "Because I'm going to give you one last choice."*

Luc woke, mid-air, falling, as he threw himself off the bed. Literally flung himself in his sleep to escape that bitch of a nightmare.

*Memory.*

God, no.

He fought for breath.

No fucking way was that a memory ... what he'd watched, what he *hadn't* done – had *allowed* to happen...

*Laughter.*

He smacked the back of his head against the floor with an angry growl, fuelled by terror, then, in a blur of motion, he rolled onto his front – onto his knees – and crawled to the wall so he could feel steady.

His back pressed into its cool solidity, and, once more, he

butted his head against it.

*In the spare bedroom ... in her house...*

That's where he was.

*...been here two days now ... you're safe.*

Safe.

Large chunks of the horrific vision were missing; pieces of some mystery he couldn't reach. The nightmare was fading, but not bloody fast enough for his liking, and...

He almost screamed. His lungs *burned* for that scream when he spied his hard-on through his newly bought boxers. In a sudden fit of desperation, he smacked that too, and then his head yet again for good measure.

What the ever-loving fuck was WRONG with him?

Something tickled his chin, and he wiped the angry tear from it against his bare shoulder, now aware that the repressed wailing filling the room was his own.

*Knocking...*

"Luc?"

*Shit, shit, shit!* He choked as he swallowed tears to try and form words. "Don't come in."

There was a pause and then, "What happened? Are you okay? I heard banging."

"Don't come in," he said again, louder – futilely. He clearly sounded distraught. He needed to offer more explanation, but they were the only three words he seemed able to summon.

He heard a soft curse from the other side of the door. Then, her voice carried through, way steadier than his. "Luc ... I'm going to come in. I'll count to ten first to give you some time."

*Fuck it.*

But he didn't hold it against her. He must have made a racket, and she had a moral obligation to ensure he was safe under her roof.

He lunged forward and grabbed the corner of the bedsheet

from where he'd strewn it across the floor when he'd leapt from the bed like a madman.

He brought his knees up, noting he was still trembling, and pulled what he could of the sheet – some of it still tucked under the mattress – across his lap. She didn't need to see *that*.

*Shouldn't have come here...*

The door opened and Evie entered, and it was strange how his trembling ceased almost immediately. His head cleared. It was as if she'd brought a rush of pure oxygen with her when she'd opened the door.

He took a deep breath in, no longer able to make out most of the dream as her presence filled the space where it had existed.

She didn't seem afraid of him.

*She should be.*

She knelt right down next to him, and a sudden image flashed through his mind of him doing the same thing – by a boy, beaten ... there were wings...

*Wings?*

"Luc."

Her voice seeped under his skin; shone a light on all the dark.

When he finally brought himself to meet her eyes, she smiled and placed a hand on his shoulder – the same one still wet with his tears.

Why wasn't she afraid? He was terrified. "Had a nightmare."

Her thumb stroked his skin. The last wisps of the dream vanished as he let out his breath.

Her presence was enough. She didn't even have to say anything. How did she do that?

He didn't know, and all at once, didn't care. Too exhausted to heed any warning, he leant forward and rested his head against her waist, and god help him, it felt like the most natural place to be in the world. He wanted to twine himself around her.

Her arms encircled him, very similar to how she'd held him at the hospital when she'd come back to him.

*She's come back...*

He couldn't muster the energy to analyse exactly what that faint whisper in his head meant.

"Everything's fine now," she mumbled into his hair.

Hadn't that been his line? Hadn't he said that to someone?

Remnants of the nightmare tried to surface, but the call of sleep was stronger. And he probably wouldn't remember it in the morning, but as slumber claimed him in the alluring warmth of Evie's embrace, the last image imprinted in his mind, was an oddly familiar one of huge, golden wings.

~*~

It wasn't until the enveloping warmth hit her, that she realised, alarmingly, she hadn't felt warmth – true warmth – for a really long time. For years. For a decade. Longer?

And that was all she could fathom at first.

Rays of winter sun bathed her face from a window that wasn't hers. But it *had* been hers, and, still mostly asleep, she smiled as awareness crept into her consciousness and brought a blanket of nostalgia with it.

*The sun?* Good god, how long had it been since she'd seen the sun? She thought it had been lost. *Better wake up and make the most of it before the clouds swallow it up again.*

The nostalgia-blanket was comforting, and the usual tinge of sadness that accompanied her occasional moments into nostalgia was absent.

She snuggled down into the beautiful warmth, and then

frowned because her bed was hard. Way harder than usual. *Really* hard.

Eyelids flickering against the morning light, she tried to get herself back to that rare state of peace, and then froze as she all at once understood the source of the warmth.

Last night's events hurtled through her mind.

Holding her breath, she peeked down the length of her body to find Luc wrapped around her tightly from behind, both of them a mass of limbs on the floor, under a single white sheet.

*What the...*

This was bad.

Was this bad?

*It feels good.*

She warmed even further at that thought, but didn't move a muscle. She could hear Luc's steady breathing behind her, feathers of air brushing against the nape of her neck with every exhale.

Heat rushed through her body starting at the centre of her womb.

Aaaand there was his cock, sporting what felt like a massive morning glory, nestling right against the crease of her backside; thin layers of cotton the only thing keeping skin from skin.

*What* was he going to say when he woke up? The last thing she wanted to do was scare him away, and he seemed to scare quite easily.

God, she daren't move. Nope. She was going to shut her eyes and let him be the first to wake.

*Coward.*

Fuck.

She remembered his distress over his nightmare, their shared embrace as she'd calmed him; she even remembered him getting heavier in her arms as he'd relaxed. She remembered thinking she should get him up and steer him back to the bed before he fell asleep, and that was *all* she remembered, before she had evidently fallen asleep, too.

*So careless...*

It hadn't escaped her notice that she did seem to lose track of time, and pretty much most things, when they were in the same room together; as if Luc was a piece of art himself, able to have that very same, dazzling effect on her. Nothing *outside* their immediate surroundings seemed to matter when they breathed air from the same shared space, and she couldn't shrug it off as the result of some strange infatuation, for it was *more* than that. It was like all matter was sucked from the room, leaving just her and him.

*You sound like an obsessed teen!*

Cringing at her inability to behave with any kind of sensibleness, she finally decided to do the grown-up thing and get up ... soon.

Real soon.

Just as soon as she shrugged the last of her sleep off ... and this delightful warmth...

*Mmmm ... don't wanna lose the warmth.*

Failed mission.

With a soft sigh, she turned, still encased in his arms, until she was lying on her back.

Her hip accidentally grazed his thick, hard shaft.

She stilled, caught her breath, and it stayed trapped in her lungs until she was sure he hadn't stirred.

*God ... he's amazing.* So amazing to look at, time did that strange thing again, sucking all existence into a vacuum as she simply gazed at him, unable to pull away. Maybe *he* was the vacuum; she was so forcefully drawn towards him, and that was no exaggeration, for before she knew it, she had propped herself up on one hand as she leaned above and over him to get a better look at his countenance, this time careful not to graze any part of him at all.

Her hair fell forwards, and she pulled back anxiously, just a little, not wanting the ends of her strands to tease his bare skin – she didn't want to wake him, not with her staring down at him like some creepy bunny boiler.

*See? Obsessed.*

Unfortunately, her movement did exactly what she didn't want, and she brushed against him once more – *that* delectable part of him – this time with the top of her right hip bone.

He moaned – a soft, male sound that sent her stomach into one mother of a somersault and her head into a spin.

*Time to get the fuck up.*

She should have seen it coming. It was déjà vu, ironised, how his eyes suddenly opened and his fingers threaded through her hair, clasping it into his fist – *just* like when she'd found him on the road – as he yanked her down against his frame, his eyes still dazed; not fully aware.

It was also *completely* different from last time, because last time, he had been injured and limp (for want of a better word) all over. Now, he was *all* steel, and god help her, his erection was right at the juncture of her thighs, her flesh wrapped around his.

Not that she should be focusing on that, but it was bloody hard not to.

She tried to swallow, not really able to ... *Fuck* – she was on fire. "Luc," she stuttered out, not really loud enough for any-one to hear, then she gasped, half in pain, as he pulled her up by her hair until her face was directly above his.

With unfocused eyes, not quite staring *at* her, he loosened his grip a little and dragged his thumb along her lip. "I remem-ber you. Like this."

*Wha...* Was he talking about when she'd found him? Did he remember?

Something on the carpet tickled her fingers.

His hand went in her hair once more, pulling, his nose brushed hers, and then he thrust, upwards, grinding his hips into hers.

A moan left her, too needy. *How* could he have such an impact on her? It was as if she was captured.

She sort of was, because wriggling out of his hold was impossible.

And then, she saw it: grass. Grass under her fingers where her carpet should be. *No...*

*Yes!* The floor was literally *morphing...*

*You're hallucinating!*

Some kind of trick of the sunlight, like when she'd seen him under the street lamp. Maybe the sensory overload wasn't helping.

With a shake of her head, and a squeeze of her eyes – shut, open – everything went back to normal. She snapped out of her irrational state. "Luc. Wake up."

Another pump of his hips had her gritting her teeth. *Jesus.* She didn't know whether to thank or curse their underwear – the only barrier preventing a very bad thing from happening.

*Not bad ... good.*

He did it again; her core like lava.

She was going to orgasm.

Alarm took over all else, and with effort, she managed to lift her left arm and slap him in the face, although she was hesitant to hurt him.

It worked.

His whole body jerked as if his muscles had spasmed, still asleep, and then his gaze lost its vacancy. He blinked. Awareness settled on his features faster than anything she'd seen.

To say he dropped her wasn't accurate. He pretty much threw her off him.

She rolled once along the floor with a small cry, as he pulled himself up and scrambled with the sheet. "What..."

"It's all right," she voiced, even though she wasn't sure it was. She was so hot – scorching hot – and she needed...

"I'm sorry," he wrenched out. His distraught tone pained her.

"Not your fault." She pulled herself up, unsure she could walk, she was so unsteady, and ... *hot*. "I'm gonna go and—"

"I'm sorry," he repeated, panicked; utterly ruined.

She shook her head as she backed out of the room. "Not your fault. You were asleep. It was an accident."

"Evie..."

"I'm gonna go wash up, then make us breakfast." She knew she was acting insane, and not throwing him the line he needed, but there was a constricting *burn* coiling around her body, reaching higher, and higher, that she couldn't shake off. Any second, it would squeeze her tight and choke her to death. "It's okay." And then she turned and speed-walked right out of there, straight into the bathroom.

Banging the door shut tight, she bolted it and her jellied legs finally gave way. They hit the cool tiles of her bathroom and after a final second trying to analyse what exactly was wrong with her, she shoved her sleep-shorts and knickers down, gasping in relief when her fingers found her centre, wet and swollen, and ... *fuck the heat.*

It didn't take long; she was on the edge, already.

Feet slammed against the base of the bath, she forced her hips up to meet her own little thrusts, back arched, and came, ferociously, hoping to hell and high waters she wasn't making a sound.

The coming back down was a sweet, sweet reward.

*What are you thinking, Evie ... what are you doing?*

Now her head had cleared from its earlier fog, she was having trouble understanding exactly what had happened. Her lack of control over her own body was embarrassing, to say the least. He just ... *did* that to her.

*Bollocks. There's no excuse.*

Shit. She needed to apologise to him for running out the way she had.

She would. She'd beg his forgiveness over jam-on-toast and coffee. He must be losing it, thinking he'd done something to her when he hadn't, but she couldn't go back into his room now – she needed to find her balance. His very presence seemed to render her useless.

Hauling herself up to sitting and pulling her hand from between her legs, she suddenly stopped, and then let out a small whimper when she noticed the blood on her fingers. Surely she hadn't hurt herself. But it couldn't be...

Looking down, shocked, she noted the red stain on her pubic hair, and must have stared at it for about a minute, trying to make logical sense of what she was seeing. *My ... period?*

But it *couldn't* be. She had been diagnosed with primary amenorrhoea from the age of eighteen, after she'd confessed to her bereavement counsellor she'd never started menstruating. A consultation with her doctor had been insisted on, but through one of the many failings of medical science, no cause for her affliction could be found. She'd had no developmental abnormalities, no trauma – physical or emotional – prior to her parents' death, and after further tests, no hormonal or genetic irregularities had been detected and it seemed her ovaries were working just fine bar the monthly malfunction.

*My first period...*

Numb, she stood, stripped off the rest of her clothes, and turned on the shower. Maybe that explained the insatiable horniness she'd had.

The blood washed off her fingers and turned the water pink as it swirled into the drain hole. Another trickle ran down her inner-thigh before it joined the mini-whirlpool.

And another.

That orgasm seemed to have really set it off.

She lifted her head to the streaming water, and soaped herself down, her thoughts turning from how she was going to have to use kitchen roll as sanitary towels until she could get to the shops, to what on earth she was going to say to Luc about the way she'd dashed out on him.

"I'm sorry," she whispered into the spray. And, all at once, she couldn't shake the feeling she was apologising for something momentous; something terrible; something catastrophic...

Tears slipped from her eyes and joined the rivulets of water jetting down her body.

Some irreparable mistake she had made.

# VIII
## *Catch*

Coffee might just be the eighth deadly sin.

Luc breathed in the seductive aroma from the top of the stairs and wondered if he'd always liked coffee.

He also wondered if he was about to get thrown out.

It didn't matter. He'd packed a bag already. The decision would be his, and he'd already made up his mind.

Facing her now after the precarious position they had found themselves in earlier was just as bad as facing everything he found horrendous about himself. Not that the feel of *her* had been horrendous – not at all. He half-hoped she wouldn't tell him what he'd done.

The other half of him wouldn't leave without knowing.

"There you are," she smiled as she spied him staring at her from the bottom step.

*Just like a creep would.*

He cleared his throat and walked forward into the open-plan, kitchen-diner, and forced himself to meet her eyes.

"I have toast, jam, marmalade, coffee, aaaaand—"

He could hear the metaphoric drum roll as she fetched a bowl from a counter behind her.

"—figs," she grinned. "Remember, I picked them up yesterday? They're perfectly ripe."

He frowned. He didn't remember that. How could he not

remember that? Surely his short-term memory wasn't going, too. "Aren't they out of season?"

He caught her own slight frown, and the way she stalled momentarily, and then, there was that smile again. "I know. Weird, huh? I was surprised to see them on the shelf. Anyway ... I love them. We can have them with honey. Or, I think I have some maple syrup somewhere..."

Her sentence trailed off, and an awkward silence filled the space between them. And he really didn't remember going to the supermarket with her at all.

"Coffee?" Evie squeaked, already reaching for the coffee jug.

"I think I should leave."

There. He'd said it.

His words dropped like lead. All colour drained from her face, and he felt like a shit.

"What?" she whispered.

"I shouldn't be here. I don't even know who I am."

"But—"

"I don't even know if I'm safe."

"Safe?"

"To be around."

"Of course you're safe."

He shook his head. "What happened earlier—"

"Was not your fault," she butted in, wide-eyed and pleading. "I was lying right there, next to you – my choice – and you were asleep."

"The fact that I was *asleep* makes it worse. If I can't even be aware of what I'm doing—"

"No." The coffee jug was slammed down on the counter.

He straightened, a little confused at her reaction.

"Stay. Please. I promised to help you find out who you are."

"And what if that takes months? Years?"

"I'm not going anywhere. Do you hate it here?"

"No – of course not."

"So, what's the problem? Look," she came out the kitchen area towards him, "I'll be better behaved, I swear. I ... this is so bloody embarrassing, but I practically put myself on top of you earlier, and I have no idea what possessed me. *I'm* the one who needs to apologise. You were just so peacefully asleep and I ... that was nice to see. *Nothing* happened. You did nothing. And I'm only sorry I ran out on you like an idiot, but I was half asleep, too, and not thinking straight."

He stood there, silently, contemplating her words.

"Where are you going to go on Christmas Eve, anyway?"

He hadn't figured out the wheres or hows.

"At least give it 'til the New Year. If you still want to go after that, then fine."

He didn't want to leave her presence, and that was the honest truth. But... "Something ... I don't know. I feel like something's missing; like something doesn't add up. Don't you think everything feels ... strange?"

"Strange? No more than usual," she laughed, quietly. "I suppose you're bound to feel like that considering the gaps in your memory."

Right. It was a damn shame he had nothing to compare *anything* to without his memory. Things felt 'odd' and he had no idea if they really were, or if it was solely down to him and his amnesia.

He glanced out the kitchen window. Rain hammered against it. "We know nothing about my life. What if I'm—"

"Married? I swear to you, nothing happened."

"No. What if I'm ... some kind of monster." He sucked in a breath, waiting for her to flinch, or something. She showed no reaction; just waited for him to expand on what he meant, and he didn't really want to, but everything he'd experienced since the hospital, plus fragments of a disturbing dream he couldn't fully remember added up to... "What if I'm dangerous? Like, a murderer, or something?"

"Luc," she rolled her eyes, "that's—"

"A possibility," he interrupted.

Annoyance crossed her features, and she turned and headed back into the kitchen.

This time, he followed.

"You're not a murderer."

"You don't know that."

"I do." She drove a knife through a fig, and peachy coloured juice seeped onto its skin. It really was ripe.

"How could you possibly—"

"Because I just *do*." She cut the fruit into quarters, her motions not without anger. "You're not a monster. Why would you even *let* anyone think that about you, let alone think it yourself."

And the weird just kept coming. This was turning into something similar to that out-of-place 'name' conversation they'd had a couple of days ago. She'd gone off on one then, too. And he had no idea what to say now, just as he'd had no idea then, for he didn't think his caution unreasonable. Sensible, yes, even if his fears turned out to be unfounded.

"Here." She held two cut up figs in both hands, and offered them to him, her fingers pink and slick from their moist core.

His mouth suddenly went dry.

His gaze travelled up past her hands, her wrists and arms, to her mouth, nose and eyes; blonde hair washed, curling around her gently oval face; irises more grey than their usual blue at this moment, emphasising her stubbornness...

God, she looked ... tempting.

The spell broke when she suddenly tutted harshly to herself, and shook her head. "What's wrong with me? You need a plate."

She turned to go find one, mumbling something about being such a daydreamer, and as she spun, wafting the air his way, a scent caught his attention, subtle, yet sharp; metallic, yet somehow ... not; caught amid the floweriness of her shampoo.

His tongue seemed to swell, all his senses heightened, and a dull ache throbbed in his gums.

*Blood.*

"Did you cut yourself?" His voice sounded from a million miles away; all his functions now on autopilot – some internal switch flicked. Fuck ... he'd been thrown from his body. *That scent.*

*Her* scent.

He *thirsted* for it.

"No, I don't think so." Her head came back into view from the low cupboard it had been in. "Plates! Hooray. Here you go."

The fruit seemed to weep red against the white of the crockery.

His stomach growled.

"Luc?"

She hadn't cut herself.

*Her cycle. She's menstruating.*

Jesus...

It wasn't the fact he could smell her most private musk that blasted him into orbit, it was the fact that he ... *craved* it.

The visual tore through him: her astride him, against him, moving... and he couldn't tell if he was creating it, or if it had happened and he couldn't remember. It didn't seem to be from that morning.

He stepped back; fire in his loins, but a deeper, more dangerous fire he didn't understand, sparked in the seat of his belly.

"Luc?"

"I have to go."

Her beautiful face looked alarmed at that. She should be alarmed – at *him*.

Another step.

"But—"

"A walk. Clear my head. I'll be back later, I promise."

"Luc!"

He ignored her cry and all but ran, desperate to shake the torturous image out of his mind, of his head buried between her legs as he drank.

~*~

*"She wasn't supposed to be there. She looked so out of place. Humans didn't quite shine like angels, but she did. Her hair gleamed like the purest gold, her blue eyes so wide and innocent; her smile lit up Eden so brightly that even if all angels had fallen from grace at once, she could have held up Heaven with her virtue alone. If I was the brightest of angels, she was the brightest of humans. Truly, she was one of God's finest creations at a time when he still adored humans as any parent should adore their children, and if God had a favourite among humans, it was surely her."*

Another dream... No – a memory... No ... a dream?

Luc twitched; desperately tried to surface from sleep. When had he fallen asleep? But he couldn't make sense of anything. All merged – illusion, reality, and all distance in between.

*"I was patrolling The Boundary when I saw her. She stood on the other side in the very pit of darkness. I called her name,*

*but she didn't hear me. Instead, she was taken by something I couldn't see; something that only the darkness could show."*

Who in the hell was he talking to? Then, as if the faceless figure heard him, he – she? – threw the question right back at him.

*"Who are you talking about, Luc?"*

Luc?

No! That wasn't what she'd called him. That wasn't his name!

His eyes snapped open.

Rain drummed the leather of his shoes. He cursed and pulled his feet in with the rest of him. Looking up, he saw that he was sheltered under a canopy in an alleyway. How exactly he'd gotten here, and when he'd fallen asleep (more to the point, *how...*) were questions he could not answer.

He was freezing and wet. When he'd dashed out of the house, he had left without taking his coat. His jumper was soaked.

Luc looked around, trying to remember anything at all of how he'd gotten here, but it was the dream that kept coming back to him, the words of which were already fading.

But his name ... what had that person called him?

Damn it, he couldn't remember.

With a sigh, he stood and focused on getting back to Evie's house. He didn't recognise a single thing, but all the houses looked similar to hers, so he hoped he was around the same area. Surely he couldn't be far.

He tried not to think about how he kept blacking out. Losing his long term memory was one thing, but losing gaps throughout the day ... that didn't bode well. Maybe he should go back to the hospital – admit himself.

He pulled a face. Voluntary torture didn't seem like his thing. He'd hold out until the first meeting with the psychologist.

The canopy he was under belonged to a small shop – antiques, or something – but it was closed.

With trepidation growing, he walked further out, right into the road, disregarding the rain hammering down on him, only to notice that *all* the shops were closed. There were only a few on this street, all small speciality stores, but all shut. It was Christmas Eve – the last Friday before Christmas – and everything was *shut*.

A shiver snaked up his spine.

*Where are all the people?*

In fact, since the hospital, he couldn't remember crossing paths with anyone at all apart from Evie.

*That can't be right. You must have at least seen people.*

He racked his brain, but drew a blank.

*Nope. Not one single person.*

Heart pounding he picked up pace until he was jogging, not really knowing where he was going, but focusing, intently, on the houses he could see.

The windows.

No one.

He couldn't see one goddamned person.

Terror held at bay, he leapt up the porch of the nearest house to him – a semi-detached, Edwardian building – and pounded on the door with the knocker.

Spying a doorbell, he rang that, too.

Thirty seconds passed.

He pounded harder. "Hello!"

Christ ... next house. And the next, and the next, for the next ten minutes that's all he did, and not a single soul emerged; not a curtain twitched.

At the end of the row of houses, he sprinted into the middle of where the two roads met. "HELLO! ANYBODY!"

His own voice bounced back at him.

Nothing stirred.

While he tried to remind himself this is how Evie said it was now, nothing added up. All the parked cars he could see were clean, the gardens and buildings were well-kept, nothing was broken, or derelict, and even though this part of town was more upmarket than some, *something* had to give. *Something* had to be out of place, and fuck, there wasn't even any litter on the streets. If this was a ghost town, the ghosts were keeping it spick and span.

*"HELLO!"* He couldn't be on his own. He didn't want to be on his own.

"Luc?"

He spun so fast he almost fell.

Evie stood before him much better prepared for the weather than he.

*"I shouldn't have crossed The Boundary, I know I shouldn't have, but I was taken with an urgency that came from the need to save her, although I didn't know what from. All I knew was that she looked so out of place..."*

"Evie..." It was *right there* at the edge of his mind, but he couldn't grasp it...

*"...she looked so out of place..."*

With the downpour moulding her raincoat to her frame, she smiled faintly, hopefully, and he wondered if she'd been crying, or if those pale tracks down her cheeks were from the rain.

She held out a hand to him. "Come on ... let's go home."

# IX
## *Penance*

**H**e doubted lamb stew had ever tasted better. And if he stayed close enough to the food, its aroma pretty much drowned out hers.

The last thing he wanted was to come off as cold and aloof, but he didn't have an awful lot to say. His head was a mess. Part of him craved isolation; part of him craved company, and as much as he wanted to see other people – *anyone* else – she was enough. More than enough. In fact, if he had to choose between never seeing anyone else again, or never seeing her again, he would choose seclusion to keep her in his life, and he didn't understand it beyond some physiological reaction to her every smile, thought and action.

Apart from the scent of her blood firing off his neurotrans-mitters (as well as other parts of his anatomy), she had a per-plexing soothing effect on his entire system. He was starting to think he might even be addicted to her, for whenever he was on his own, he felt on the verge of panic, began hallucinating, or having nightmares, and trembling from all three. Talk about getting the DTs. And he didn't even want to think about his passing out earlier.

It didn't make him feel any better about his serial killer theory, though. Perhaps this was how serial killers became at-tached to their targets.

At least he could rule out drugs (or their withdrawal) as a cause of his responses. The reports at the hospital had all stated no narcotics had been found in his bloodstream, although a larger-than-usual amount of cyanide had been detected in his urine. Hardly enough for his symptoms to be the result of cyanide poisoning, and none had been evident in his blood or tissues after further tests.

*So ... it really is all in your head.*

Yeah. That wasn't good news either.

"I don't know why I didn't see it coming with Philip, but I've always been that way with people." Evie chirped away happily, despite his silence, seemingly just relieved to have him back. "I think it's me. It's got to be. When people let you down again and again, you've got to look at the lowest common denominator. I think I just expect too much; have too much hope, or something." She reached for the pot of stew in the centre of the table. "Would you like any more?"

"Oh ... no, thanks. It's delicious, but I'm full. And I don't think there's anything wrong with being hopeful."

She made a cute, small snorting sound as she served herself seconds. "Maybe losing your memory's a good thing. No, really. With amnesia, you can kind of start anew; pretend nothing's the way it really is."

"And how is it, really?"

"In this world, people like to tear down the hopeful ones." She shrugged, her cheeriness now tainted with a hint of sadness, all the more sad because her acceptance of her sorrow seemed damaging somehow, as if she truly believed the world could not be changed. "It's ... hopeless." She looked down and swirled her food with her fork.

"If you lose hope, mankind loses hope."

Her movements stilled, and he had no idea where on earth that had come from.

He coughed to clear his throat, and the odd ring of truth that clung to the air from his words. "I mean, people – you, as in *people*. If people lose hope, what is there left?"

She lifted her eyes to meet his. They shone with tears, which disappeared after two blinks, and then, she abruptly dropped her fork, all smiles once more. "I have something for you." She stood and disappeared into the other room.

He shuffled uneasily in his chair, unsure if he really wanted to accept anything else from her. She'd given him so much already, but an uncomfortable question was starting to creep into his psyche: *why?*

What did she gain out of this? Did she have an ulterior motive?

His trust of her felt deep – as if he knew her; as if it spanned lifetimes – but for the first time, his amnesia aside, he was getting the inkling things weren't as they should be. At all.

This was a beautiful, big house with white walls, decorated to be airy and breezy, and yet the weight of depression clung to it that seemed more than her loneliness. *What ghosts are you suppressing?* he asked her, silently.

Evie reappeared through the doorway carrying a present wrapped in Christmas wrapping paper. "Um…" she began, shyly, "I know nothing looks Christmassy here – no tree, no decorations. I sort of haven't bothered too much with living on my own, but I didn't want you to feel left out just 'cause I'm sad," she laughed. "Here … it's just a little thing." She placed it in front of him and took her seat again.

He glanced at her, surprised. "You didn't have to do that."

"I know. I wanted to. I know Christmas is tomorrow, but it just seemed like the right time to give it to you now – besides, you might need it for tomorrow." Another laugh.

She was trying so hard, and he felt like a bit of a dick for not jumping into her enthusiasm. He gave her a small smile, and slipped his finger into a gap in the wrapping to tear it. "Thank you."

She grinned and watched as he peeled away the paper.

It was a shirt. An elegant-looking white one with embroidered twines of branches and leaves sewn in silver thread, meandering from the hem to the collar and along the sleeves, too.

"I think I got your size right. If not, I can change it."

"It's ... really lovely. I don't know what to say."

"Would you like to try it on?"

Confusion washed over him. "Where ... when ... did you buy this?"

"Just a couple of days ago."

So vague... "Evie, I didn't see any shops open when I was out earlier. I haven't seen a single person. Anywhere." He looked at her, gauging her reaction.

She visibly swallowed hard, and then the smile was back. "I told you, that's just the way it is now. You have to know where to go and when to catch the shops open."

He didn't buy it. But with no memory of these quakes and how everything became this way, he hadn't a clue how to argue his case.

Looking at the shirt once more, he caught sight of something glimmering under the ceiling lights: cufflinks. Fingering them, something clicked in his mind as he examined the small, silver-plated apples that decorated the bottom of each sleeve... *Apples...*

"How weird," mumbled Evie, now looking white as a sheet. "I could have sworn they were leaves – not ... that."

"You mean the apples?"

She looked faint. Her next attempted smile wavered and she stood, clearing the plates.

"I do like it. Really. I'll go try it on."

"No. I mean ... there's no rush. Nothing will be open tomorrow anyway, so maybe just try it on tomorrow."

The oddity of that suggestion lay mainly in the fact that he'd seen nothing open *today*. Her colour had not returned, either. He decided to go out on a limb. "You are telling me everything, aren't you? About how you found me, and why I'm here?"

Evie stood still as a statue. Too still. She had that wide-eyed look truly mastered. She was innocence personified. "Of course. What else would there be?"

A question he couldn't answer, and she knew it.

With nothing to go on, he briefly closed his eyes and took a deep breath in, placing instinct alone into the gap his memory created. He had nothing else.

Bottom line: he trusted her not to hurt him. And although he didn't know why, it was all he had to go on, so that's what he went with.

Was she keeping something from him?

Yes. He was sure.

Was it for his own safety? Maybe. But everything in him told him her intention was not to harm him.

He let his breath out, and then nodded. "I'm going to go upstairs and hang this shirt up."

"Okay," Evie whispered in reply.

"Thanks, again."

"You're welcome."

~*~

She turned towards the sink, trembling, as Luc's footsteps sounded on the stairs.

*Oh god oh god oh god...*

Something was wrong with her; she was seeing things ...

first the grass in place of her carpet that morning, and then the leaf cufflinks which had turned out to be apples – how? She had definitely bought leaves. She hated apples.

*And what about those wings, when you first saw him?*

On top of that, she wasn't feeling herself. Subduing her ridiculous obsession with Luc was proving more than difficult. In fact, it seemed that every time he was around she lusted after him more and more, and became a stuttering fool. She couldn't even leave him be for a few hours – as soon as he'd disappeared for that walk earlier, she had paced and fidgeted, and then finally had *had* to go find him.

*It's your period.*

She exhaled sharply, an unexpected anger surging. *Might as well do what everyone does and blame that time of the month – as if it's a disease, or a curse. As if it somehow offers an out; special compensation for craziness.*

She wasn't just angry, she was *seething*, the irrational rage seated behind her diaphragm seeming out of place with the simplicity of her surroundings; a wave of violence washing over her. It came and went quickly – that flash of a kill; some baseless, murderous intent, bathed in red – and then, it was gone, and she was looking at the dinner left over on the table.

Suddenly weary, anger faded, she walked over to the table to clear up. The lamb would keep for another day.

She picked up the pot, turned, then recoiled in horror as white fleece lay heavy in her arms – the dish gone – wool still attached to the warm body of the young animal, seeping red in the blood of its sacrifice.

With a piercing scream, she dropped the dead lamb, but it was the pot that smashed into pieces on hitting the ground.

She heard the heavy pounding on the stairs as Luc raced down them. "Eve!"

*What do I say to him? What do I say?*

"Evie," she corrected him, automatically, her voice too small and shaking. *Liar...*

She looked away from the dinner on the floor, and fixed her gaze on his.

Perhaps, they were both monsters.

~ * ~

Everything was fine until *the possibility.*

Possibility was a seed, and a strong one at that. It needed the care of the rain, the will of the sun, and it could grow, untethered, into a reality.

The seed grew in Evie as she dreamt...

*...dark, unknown, and beautiful for it – the alluring forbidden. Temptation only existed because of the forbidden. But denying herself seemed also a sin. She was the explorer, the adventurer, the artist and the creator. She always had been. She loved to create. It was how her Father had made her, so how could He expect her be any other way but true to her own calling?*

*Gods were as flawed as men.*

*Something had been missing. She had always known it, although the feeling had no name and no logic. She was a fragment – created incomplete.*

*"Lilith!" she screamed, urgency driving her on.*

*God was going to destroy it all.*

*She had seen the darkness on the other side of The Boundary, and the darkness had held a light brighter than anything she'd ever seen. Therein lay her completion – the lost piece she'd been searching for. Every time she ventured across The Boundary, she remembered something crucial. Perhaps more amazing, this blanket of darkness held true magic, for here,* she could be the artist she craved to be; she could mould the darkness into something material and create solid things to represent those missing pieces – not something she could do on the light side of Eden.

But her last creation – a beautiful statue of the one called Lilith who lived in the darkness – her Father had condemned.

And now, he was angry.

Evie moaned in her sleep...

She looked back out towards the light, catching sight of a majestic, Edwardian house in the distance, roads filled with cars and people... She blinked – no people. Blinked again – people. No people, people, no people, people...

You should go back out there, whispered her inner-voice.

No people.

She wasn't one of them. The sorrow that realisation brought was crushing... You were never good enough for them.

The night forest rustled behind her.

She turned back to the darkness to see a figure in the distance, behind a tree – a woman – hair so long and black it merged with the dark surrounding her, making it seem as if her shadowy aura was infinite; as if she encompassed the entire world.

This side of it, anyway.

But unlike Evie, this woman was not solid, but barely a wisp of the shadows she lived in.

Lilith!

Mother... whispered her mind, although she couldn't properly grasp the meaning of the word, just like all those fragments of herself she couldn't quite remember.

Not understanding the depth of her thoughts and feelings, Evie gravitated towards her, trying to dim her confusion.

Father told me I was the only woman... made from man.

*Further words formed in her mind, coming directly from Lilith as she disappeared behind a tree. "I am not made of man."*

*Evie stalled, shocked, because this was a solid tree. She didn't think she had once seen anything 'solid' in Eden, other than herself, Adam, and the creations she liked to conjure that she was now paying the price for.*

*The explorer in her fully awakened, she followed at a greater speed, not wanting to lose the being she knew could give her answers to questions not yet thought of.*

*As the tree loomed above her, she took it in with slight awe. Gleaming balls of fruit she had never seen before hung from the low branches. "I had no idea fruit could grow in the dark."*

*"Only by venturing into the dark can you possibly know what it bears."*

*She shivered at Lilith's voice, so close to her. "Does Father know this tree is here?"*

*Her long tresses came into view from behind the trunk, until she stood before her. "Your Father is afraid of the dark, and will not step foot in it. It is his downfall. I won't let it be mine, and neither should you."*

*"I've made him so angry," she blurted out, her earlier panic rising. "I just wanted to remember you, so I thought of you and my thoughts made you manifest before His eyes, in some solid matter not unlike that of a tree, and now he knows you exist and that I crossed The Boundary, and he is raging, and I fear he will destroy you."*

*She remained calm in the face of Evie's agitation. "Darkness cannot be destroyed."*

*"I don't understand."*

*"Have you not felt as if something is missing, Eve?"*

Evie stirred...

"No matter where you look, or how hard you try, there is this void – unfillable – this chasm of constant yearning."

Her eyes widened in amazement. Never had any being given voice to her needs so succinctly.

"Dark and light need to be merged, Eve – never separated. That is the cause of the yearning, and look what God – your Father – has done. Created The Boundary and there is no undoing it ... at least, not yet – not until serpents grow wings once more. But what we cannot undo from the outside, we can undo from within."

"How?"

The woman smiled. "Know, Eve. Know thyself."

"I do."

"You know only half of yourself." She pointed at the fruit growing overhead. "Take one."

Reaching up, Evie picked one of the round yields, and stared at it, curiosity piqued. Its colour was one she had never seen before, but it was seductive to say the least. It made her body hum.

"This is an apple," said Lilith.

"Apple," she repeated, the word foreign to her ears.

"It holds duality within its core – duality merged. It will show you your deepest desires. Your secret wants and wishes."

"Desires? I ... I have no..." She'd been about to say she had no desires, but sudden clarity flooded her mind. Why should her Father be the only one allowed to forge great things, when her urge for doing the same was just as forceful? He had made her in his image. *She was also an artist.* "I desire to create."

Lilith smiled. "I want you to split the apple in half down the stalk, then hold both halves open."

*She did as instructed, using her nails and was surprised the fruit separated so easily.*

*"What do you see?" asked Lilith.*

*She inspected both parts, then after a pause, shook her head. "I don't know. Just two halves, I suppose."*

*Lilith grinned, a faint flash of teeth gleaming. "Good. And look in one of the halves."*

*She did. The fruit showed two adjacent, connected, oval-shaped quarters with a seed embedded in each quarter.*

*Lilith took a step towards her. "Place the fruit against you, low upon your belly, and hold it there."*

*She did as instructed, pressing the fruit-half against her navel, its juicy inside against her skin.*

*"Two. Always two. The apple is the fruit of life; of the first breath. Now, take another."*

*Eve picked another apple from the tree and this time, was told to split it from side to side, rather than top to bottom.*

*"Good. Now, look again, for the apple is a fruit of the shadows with many layers; many stories to tell."*

*Five points – five seeds – stared back at her in the shape of—*

*"A star!" smiled Evie. "Like the faint rays of the Morning Star."*

*"Faint? Goodness, no." Lilith was as close as could be now, wafting around her like smoke, only her touch was as cold as ice. "Have you ever seen a star whilst standing in the dark?"*

*Her heart sped up a beat. "No," she whispered.*

*The woman's eyes filled with tears. "And neither have I, for too long." She composed herself, took in a shuddering breath, and then encouraged Evie to raise the fruit to her mouth. "Why don't you take a bite?"*

*Alarm bells went off.*

*It wasn't that she didn't want to – she did; craved the*

apple's fresh, crisp scent even, as it danced across her tongue. It was that this was a dream, or a memory, and this had already come to pass.

The vision of a hospital flashed before her eyes. Was that the present? Was that now? And this was ... then?

"Something bad will happen. I remember..." God, no! She didn't want to remember!

You're dreaming! Wake up!

"Don't go," said Lilith, a desperate edge to her tone. "Not yet. Just one bite. There is nothing to be afraid of – this has already happened."

Evie looked back the way she'd come in. It was barely visible through the trees and the dark, but she could see her safe, white house in the distance.

"Please... I am not one for pleading, so do not take my words lightly." Lilith's see-through fingers traced a line down Evie's jaw. "You deserve freedom. Do not let your fear and hate bind you the way your Father has. I have loved you both – I still do. Bite."

Tears blurred her vision as she backed away, dropping the apple.

Defeat slumped Lilith's shoulders. "You fear to remember? You fear a ghost?"

"I fear the pain."

"You fear pleasure."

"I am not allowed pleasure."

"That is them *talking* – not you."

"I am *them*. I am them and they are me."

"A mother gives birth and, when the time is right, lets her children go. The time is right now."

"Who will I be without them? I don't know who I am."

"And you never will unless you bite."

"Evie..."

*She jumped at the sound of her name reaching her from afar. Light cut through the dark – his light, so very bright amid the blackest of black. She stilled, smiling, the hairs on her skin rising, her heart leaping for joy. Was* this *what a star looked like in the dark?*

*He was looking for her? Beautiful angel. He had always looked out for her; had always protected her. He had always been her favourite among the angels. Where most angels regarded her as a bit of an anomaly, he admired her zest for exploration and shared her curiosity of all things. His spark seemed so much brighter than that of other angels, and unlike other angels, he appeared able to detach from the order of things, and they had shared a few adventures together because of this, not minding or caring that their forms were so different. If Father minded, he had not said, and she was grateful, for he was her only true friend. Lucifer understood her – more so than Adam. She and Adam fought over most things.*

*Her smile faded.*

*Lucifer shouldn't be here ... he'd crossed The Boundary! Because of her? Oh, no...*

Your fault...

*"Bite, Eve!"*

Everything that happens next is your fault. Everything.

*Fear won.*

*It sent a shot of adrenaline into her system, and she fled, back towards the terraced house in the familiar street.*

*"You can't run from what has already been!"*

*That's not what she was running from. She was running from what was to come.*

"Evie... Wake up..."

*Here. It was already here.*

*Caught in between the past and the future; in the web of grey between light and dark.*

*No way out now.*

# X
## *Blood*

"**E**vie... Wake up..."

*You shouldn't be here.* That had become his mantra; the never-ending taunt in his head from a voice that grew louder each time it chimed. But he'd had another fucker of a nightmare, this one of her, and although it had faded on opening his eyes, as it always did, he remembered Evie, standing in darkness, an apple in one hand, a scream in her heart, and no matter how fast he flew towards her, she was no nearer at all.

When he'd woken, he'd woken to her cry. Her very *real* cry coming from the next room.

Stumbling in the black of night, he had pummelled into her room and dove onto her bed, fright still snapping at his heels.

She thrashed in her sleep, her covers flapped, and that was the moment he realised his grave mistake, for her blood-scent hit him like a freight train – so hard he felt winded – and by god ... floating on the top of her intimate aroma, he swore he caught the trail of ... *apples.* As if the fruit were somehow in her system, entwined with her blood.

Why that affected him so, he couldn't say, but it sent his head into a spin he couldn't shake off, so he shook her instead, one hand on each arm, perhaps to wake her; perhaps to keep his own grip on reality... "Evie... *Wake up.*"

Rain hammered her window, the sky sobbing with angry grief, and a flash of silent lightning lit the sky far off in the distance. It was enough to draw his attention to the anomaly he caught out of the corner of his eye – out the window.

With caution, he rose, leaving a still-dreaming Evie whimpering on the bed, and made his way to the pane.

His veins ran cold as the glow of the street lamp across the road cast its light on a blooming apple tree, ripe with fruit, growing from the drain that covered the hole in the road. The same drain he'd been found caught in.

*You're still dreaming,* said his inner-voice of reason, far too weakly.

"No," he answered, his breath steaming the glass in front of him. "I'm not."

Evie's scream scarred the walls, and Luc was back by her side, her glassy eyes wide with both rage and fear as she bolted upright. Her duvet fell to her waist, revealing unclothed breasts, beautifully round and perfectly tipped with dusky-rose nipples.

For a moment, he was entranced, as if he'd never seen the female form before in his life, until her palm smacked against the side of his neck in a death-grip so brutal he hissed at the contact.

"I won't remember! I won't!"

Her nails cut into his skin and drew blood. His own scent spiced the air along with hers and made him weak. Gums, groin, feet, head – his entire being ached with furnaced need he couldn't put a name to. *You shouldn't be here...*

For a second, all fell silent except for the drumming of the rain.

Evie's eyes cleared, understanding rising with waking consciousness. They focused on him, startled. "You shouldn't be here," she whispered.

The ground rumbled as if in agreement.

She looked down at her carpet; at the tremors. "The quakes..." Her words trailed off. And then she looked all around with confusion painted over her face, her eyes settling on the window. "Do I know this place?"

He risked a glance out the window himself, and spotted nothing where that tree had stood a minute ago. But he was starting to get used to his unreliable vision in this uncertain version of reality.

Evie's trembling, soft voice snaked under his skin. "I don't know who I am. I'm losing my mind." Her hand slipped from his neck and trailed down his chest, leaving thin lines of deep red from where his blood had pooled under her nails. "I did this to you."

Lord give him strength, he was on the brink of something dangerous. All he could smell was him, and her, and a ghost of the musk their merged scents would create. "You did nothing to me."

"I hurt you."

"You saved me."

An apple fell from the ceiling and landed by his left foot.

And then another, and another. It was raining apples.

With an illogical calm – because this was no stranger than anything else – he leaned down and picked one up.

A memory finally stirred; so embedded in chaos it was, that he squeezed his hand around the fruit to keep a hold of it.

The apple crushed in his hand... *Strength...* Its juice seeped from his fist... *Power...* A light ignited in his soul... *Knowledge...*

"Now, I'm going to save you."

Save her from what, he wasn't sure, but *saving her* was something he knew he had to do, so before she could protest, he covered her mouth with his juiced palm: the apple was the key.

She turned her head, eyes wide with shock, struggled, her mouth opening automatically in objection. He felt her tongue flick the centre of his hand and then she swallowed in an attempt to breathe.

Every inch of him was hard with heat.

*Here it is – the monster you knew you were...* But the painful declaration was only a faint murmur amid blood and fruit. His hand dropped and he dove on her mouth with his own, licking, sucking and tasting every bit of pulp that slipped down her lips and chin.

History unravelled.

An aeon of it.

Every memory from every dynasty of every century flooded his cells. With a furious growl, he pushed her hard into her bed.

Matching his fury, she slapped him across the face.

"Ouch, my love." Grabbing her upper arms, he pinned her beneath him.

She bucked; tried to throw him off with her legs, but he had her securely bound with the weight of his whole body.

"No!" she cried, her stricken protest cutting through acts that could not be undone.

He knew full well the seat of her suffering – *remembered it* – and the agent of her fight. "Too late," he replied, "by a thousand ages and a day."

His lips found her neck and she gasped, still writhing and wild.

He was also wild – with need and lust and longing older than time. His tongue flitted across her left nipple and she moaned a sound of both desire and defeat as the nub grew erect from his touch. "Why like this?" he said suddenly, grief spearing through need. "You took my mind prisoner. You took everything I knew."

"Not just *your* mind. You think you know what it is to be a prisoner?"

"You took my—"

"I took nothing! I've only just remembered."

"You forgot?"

"Forgot? The peace of that escape is one never afforded me for long. I can *never* forget – I'm never allowed." And then, her own grief cut through all fury. "I *ruined* you."

Her pain became his, like it always had. "I *chose*." His mouth closed around her right breast, that nipple was just as agreeable to the caress of his tongue as the other.

Another moan of want left her, her need comparable to his, yet bitter rage at memories too fresh – too raw – still permeated them both. She fought and jerked. "You were deceived."

"Only those who do not wish to see can be deceived. You deceive yourself now." He licked a trail down, between her breasts, stopping to lavish her belly button, her taste filling his mind with visions of the first time. With her. Although those archaic images were few and far between, for if she had never been allowed to forget, he had never been allowed to remember – not *that* moment. But what he did remember, was that nothing and no one had ever compared to her, and now she was here, with him, flesh against flesh...

"Lucifer..." she breathed sharply, as his kiss landed on her mound, her dark, rich spice devouring him ... for an eternity, devouring him.

"Eve," he muttered, her sensual carnality igniting all of creation.

He remembered chasing her as the world fell apart. And then the hospital, the visions, the inconsistencies of the material ... none of which completely made sense, but *she* did. Her –

the feel of her – made perfect sense.

Razor sharp pain sliced his back, and he groaned as his wings exploded, red-gold wonders filling the room which continued to tremble around and beneath them.

Control hanging by a thread, his nose pressed into her soft tuft of hair and he reached forward to taste more of her – her very essence – all of Earth in her pulse.

Her covetous cry split the universe. Her legs lifted; parted for their forbidden pleasure and where once, all was lost...

All was found.

~*~

*A shadow loomed from her left. "She's not yours, betrayer..." Just a whisper, for He – her Father – never dared cross The Boundary. But it was a whisper that held all of Eden in its notes.*

*She sobbed, holding everything that existed in her arms, knowing in an instant it would exist no more.*

*Lucifer stirred awake against her breast, the man and angel in him reigning where the serpent had before, and she could see his confusion.*

*"She's not yours."*

*Lucifer startled at His presence. "No..."*

*She held him as tight as she could.*

*Him. Hers.*

Mine.

*"Eve will fall bound to Adam. She will answer to Adam. She will never forget..."*

*Eden shook. The ground split.*

*"And you, betrayer, will fall alone and never remember."*

*"No!" she screamed.*

*"Eve!" Lucifer's wings rose in a protective shield, his eyes*

*wild with confusion. Her angel was lost; his purity deceived through her – her fault.*

*Rage shook her as ferociously as the rock under her swayed, and with it came Lilith's voice and a vision, basked in the crisp scent of apples, of countless men and countless women; of eyes wide shut...* "This will happen once more. Then and only then, will all things fallen rise, and all things sleeping wake. Know who you are..."

*Urgency lashing, Eve stretched out beneath Lucifer and reached for the apple with her left hand. Her finger brushed it, and then her hand clasped around it. She brought it up to his lips.* "I'm so sorry," *tears streamed,* "I wanted to find something I'd lost. This fruit shows you your deepest desires. It was Adam's undoing, mine, and that of Eden, but it can be what saves you. Know yourself, Lucifer. Know your desires and know what mankind truly desires, or man will forever be lost because of my mistake. They have no one to guide them now. Be their light. Bite."*

If only the snake hadn't been the first to bite.

The world fell down.

Her ceiling, her walls, her very existence, crumbling ... ashes to ashes, dust to dust.

And Lucifer moved – drank – like a man dying of thirst; her blood his milk, her body his bread in this mergence of past and present.

Grass grew up between her fingers where she clutched at the ground – bed gone. She reached for him, untamed between her legs, and twined her fingers through his hair.

The *feel* of him ... she'd *never* forgotten. "Angel of mine..."

Never forgotten...

"Have you ever seen a star whilst standing in the dark?"

Her heart sped up a beat. "No," she whispered.

Lilith's eyes filled with tears. "And neither have I, for too long." She composed herself, took in a shuddering breath, and then encouraged Eve to raise the fruit to her mouth. "Why don't you take a bite?"

Her vision blurred as she tore her gaze from Lucifer's light, to the apple in her hand.

"Bite, Eve!"

Her wonder at Lucifer's presence turned to horror. For her to have broken the sacred rule and crossed The Boundary was one thing, but for an angel to do so... "No. He isn't supposed to be here."

"He chose."

"Out of duty to my well-being."

"Still a choice. All who cross The Boundary into the dark seek something, just as you do."

"He seeks me!"

Lilith stared at her, unwavering. "Yes," she uttered, quietly. "Perhaps he does."

Anger surfaced as she fixed her eyes once more on his light, still too far in the distance. Unlike her – a human – he had no form. But he was not like Lilith either.

Angels existed as shining beings that reflected thought and emotion. They were purity refracted across Heaven, and no other more than Lucifer, the brightest star of them all. The blackness they stood in would taint him forever. "I will leave now. I will leave with him. I will not return."

A sad, almost arrogant smile graced Lilith's features. "You cannot ignore what screams to be heard. The gaping hole in you, small though it may be now, will grow, and grow, until it consumes you to sate its hunger. Open your mind, Eve, or your mind will drive you mad for it knows what it is and what *it wants. It knows what's missing.* You need to create.

"*God cut existence in two. Until duality becomes one again, you cannot live hiding from the dark and all that you crave. You must see it,* accept *it, for any way it can, the dark will seek you out for that acceptance, just as you sought it out when you stepped foot into my land – my shadowed half of Eden to which I'm bound until your Father overthrows his own insanity,*" she spat out, heaving. "*Eve...*" The apple was brought up to her mouth once more, gone from her own hand and now sitting on Lilith's palm despite her intangible state. "*Accept the darkness and your desires. Take them into you. You will save yourself much pain if you are the first to bite.*"

*If one had no choice but to disobey their Mother or their Father, which should it be? Which inflicted hurt would carry less harm?*

*She worried over it too long.*

*Lucifer's light became blinding and filled the darkness white – painful white – and although angels had no voice, she heard his cry of agony as if it had ripped from her own lungs. Panic for his safety overtook all else.* "What have you done?" *she screamed at Lilith.*

*Before her eyes, Lucifer's light disappeared, blackness taking its place, and for miles, nothing but blackness.*

*Extinguished.*

"What have you DONE?"

*Lilith's shoulders sagged as she let out a soft breath.* "Nothing, Eve. I do not control the dark any more than it controls me. The hard way it is, then."

*A quiet 'thump' sounded on the grass beneath her feet, and Eve spied the apple, dropped from Lilith's translucent grasp.*

*She lunged at it, unable to hold tears at bay for whatever had befallen her angel, rammed the hard fruit against her teeth and bit.*

"*Too late, daughter. The snake was the first to bite, so tempting was the angel's light. The serpent seeks its wings, brutally torn from its bone when all existence was severed in half, and until the serpent finds them, your angel is now bound to its form. He shall be its eyes, its ears, its scales as it scours the ground. And the wings it yearns for.*"

*Eve heard her, but wasn't listening.*

*The fruit fell from her two hands as a great weight bore upon her.* "*I feel... What's happening?*" *All her senses sharpened in a way she'd never known; prickles danced upon her skin like small, demonic stars with blades for points, and everything went ... down.*

*Eve rode out a moan as heavy heat surged through her body...* Down. "*My body...*"

"*Is even more that it was before. Did you think yourself perfected? Welcome to sensation. Welcome to lust, anger, envy – the shadows of love, passion and acceptance.*"

*Fire shot between her legs, leaving her breathless and...*

*Shocked, she reached down with her hand to feel the slick, bright-coloured wet that stained the flesh of her thighs. The same colour as the apple.* "*What is this?*"

"*Blood.*"

"*What is blood?*"

*Lilith met her stare and held it.* "*Your identity. Your uniqueness, your singularity, your integrity ... your Self. Everything your Father has denied you for favour of his fear, and to keep you safe from what he perceives to be harm. Blood is the gift of life – the gift of the Creator. We, as incomplete beings of Eden and Heaven cannot carry it, but you...*" *She crouched next to Eve on the ground, levelling with her, dropping her tone.* "*You can now carry us* all *– from either side of The Boundary – into a new existence.*"

*Something crashed along the undergrowth.*

*Lilith looked up, startled, as did Eve.*

*A creature emerged, much larger than herself and just as solid as that tree – some monstrous chimera, surely, for it looked half man and half things-that-ought-not-be-spoken-of.*

*Lilith sucked in a sharp breath, standing, stepping backwards, her expression one of awe and trepidation combined. "What happens next, I do not know. This is a secret only for you – the one who carries Genesis – and for," she stared warily at the beast, "the one who brings the New Dawn."*

*"Lilith?" she stuttered out, her voice shaking, eyes still on the deformed creature as she silently pleaded for her illusive mentor to stay – not to leave her in this God-forsaken place.*

*She disappeared; into thin air it seemed, and with a small whimper of fear, Eve fixed her focus on the monster within a yard of her now.*

*Its slitted eyes were cemented on that 'blood' between her legs. A tongue, split in two like Eden itself, emerged from its scaly mouth and flicked at the air as if tasting it.*

*The animal shuddered, then writhed in some silent battle with itself. Suddenly, its skin cracked, shedding a layer, and Eve all but wept as magnificent wings broke through its long body, feathers carrying this new colour of her blood, and the brightest gold of the twin suns that protected the skies of Eden.*

*From its hiding place, a whole male form emerged, muscled and defined and far taller than Adam – the only other male form she'd ever seen.*

*But scales still clung to half his body as he gazed at her, confused and bewildered, eyes still slitted and the blackest of blacks while he fought for control of his body and mind. "Eve?" His voice croaked, as dry as the serpent's skin he'd shed. "What's happening? Are you ... all right?"*

*Am I... Realisation cut her, its steel far too sharp.* Oh. Dear.

Heaven... "*Lucifer?*" It was him – it was – she could see it clearly; his light was still there, simply hidden.

*He had become ... solid. Manifest. Made man.*

*Now she wept.*

*Tears cascaded as she reached for him, her angel, no less beautiful for his new condition because she knew him well, and he would never hurt her in a million ages ... unlike her.* "I did this to you," she sobbed, uncontrollably.

He crawled into her space and took her into his arms, looking upon his material form in stunned silence.

But his touch was both the devil and the saint. Something she couldn't name jolted through her as skin met skin, and there was that bearing down again ... heat, fire... *What name had Lilith given it?*

Lust.

*A low rumble sounded in Lucifer's chest, which rested against her ear. Wetness seeped from the place between her thighs where all aches seemed to gather.*

*More blood? Or something else?*

*Lucifer's hand wrapped around hers and he lifted it to his lips, her fingers still coated with her life-gift. Or was it a curse?* "You did nothing to me. I chose. Your hurt is my hurt. It always has been." *He licked the taint from her flesh.*

She placed her other hand around his neck, caressed his face, his solid chest, in wonderment. But it was dread that reigned. "We've done something terrible," she whispered, afraid.

"Impossible," he replied.

"How so?"

"Because I know you, and you are incapable of terrible things."

Her eyes filled with tears anew as her heart soared, yet sank, at his words. He had always been so caring of her. "And I *know you, Lucifer. I know you. Even surrounded by eternal night, all I see is your light."*

*His lips brushed hers.*

*She gasped and pulled back as her mouth tingled, almost painfully, that same 'thing' jolting through her; the air itself seeming to come alive between them... In nurture, or in punishment? "I'm on fire," she uttered, softly, wondering if it were actually true. "I feel like I must be one of the suns. These bodies scare me. The fruit..." She brought his hand, still holding hers, down to her belly. "I feel it here."*

*"You ate it?"*

*She nodded. "And you were bitten by a snake." She smoothed her finger over a patch of scales on his arm.*

*"What is a 'snake'?"*

*"I heard they are the shadows of the Dragons that once reigned. I thought they were myth. I thought many things I've found here on this side of The Boundary were myth. Does it hurt? The bite?"*

*He frowned, became still, and Eve knew he was focusing on the feel of his new form, trying to decipher one ache from the next, and what constituted 'pain' in this unfamiliar physique. She felt the same. Many parts of her pulsed with new soreness – sometimes sharp, and sometimes sweet.*

*He took her hand from her belly and brought it towards himself, then wrapped her fingers around the hard flesh that protruded from between his legs.*

*She took in a sharp breath as he let his out. "It hurts here," he replied, his voice thick and breaking with ... she didn't know what, but it stoked her own aches – made that missing piece inside her she'd been searching for since forever, a dangerous cavern that stole her ... identity.*

*She tightened her grip on him, he groaned loudly, and she pulled him back towards her until his mouth met hers once* more.

He wept from his shaft, under her palm, and she startled at the thought that she'd hurt him, but he wrapped his hand firmly around hers, pressed her soft skin against his hardness, now glistening with wet, and moved her hand along it; up, down...

An "oh" escaped her; then with a sound from his being, like rock breaking, he collided with her again; lips on lips, clashing teeth and tongues entwining.

Words fled her.

Only sensation existed.

And that missing piece.

His mouth and hands stroked her skin, everywhere, anywhere, as did hers on him – tasting; the sweet pain traversing her being, and culminating between her thighs, bloomed until it became too much and Eve cried out an agonising sound of a need she couldn't name, but that Lucifer seemed to understand all the same.

He crushed her against him and hauled her upwards until she straddled where he sat on the ground, his wings fully extended.

The seat of all her hurt met the head of his swollen skin, and he moaned against her lips, his agony clearly as great as hers.

Perhaps he was the cure for her strange, new, bleeding wound.

That's what this felt like – a cure, within grasp, but just out of reach – and as she instinctively pressed herself down onto him, they both groaned loudly, wildly; his penetration of her both torturous and indescribably wonderful.

She sank all the way down the length of his flesh, the feeling of complete fullness – completion! Finally! – *blindingly beautiful.*

*Tears of joy, and an unfamiliar 'overwhelm', racked her heart as something else racked her body from within, pushing her to move against her ever-giving angel in search of the crest of that fullness.*

"Eve," *he whispered, urgently and brokenly, as she did as her body bade her and rocked on the seat of her lover.*

Lover.

*Yes! Surely that was the right word. If she – and man – was a physical manifestation of God, surely what physically happened between man could only be a manifestation of love, for God was love, was He not?*

Oh, how innocent she had been!

Lucifer's not a man, *corrected her mind.*

*But he had been made one, at least in form. Because of a bite.*

*Her eyes landed on the apple that had fallen from her grasp.*

Because of what you desire ... you did this to him, not God...

*Just as guilt came close to invading her once more, her angel said her name again, and it was like magic – to hear her name from the soul of one who adored her; one whom she adored in return; one who mirrored her every emotion and comprehended every feeling she emanated.* "You've always understood me," *she muttered into his mouth, still revelling in the taste of him.* My missing piece.

*For a second she froze, clarity hitting her full force.*

*She'd known.*

*Of course she had known, but she had never once entertained the idea, for she was human and he was not. She had form and he had existed beyond form. He was angel. He was* out of her reach – had been. He was forbidden.

But it had never been Adam. While she had been created to temper Adam's wildness, she had found her own wildness adrift with no anchor, and no validation.

Here was her anchor – Lucifer.

It had never been Adam.

And the way her angel gripped her as he moved inside her...

Her wildness billowed into a tempest – anarchic; violent; hazardous – yet she had never felt more safe, her ballast in her arms, and paving a way through the centre of her being.

Lucifer's opulent wings trembled, and he emitted his light – his glow – just as angels did, but this time, instead of the bright white light it had been, it was a regal, golden glow that rivalled that of the twin suns that ruled Eden's sky.

She basked in it.

But his eyelids suddenly flickered and his irises altered, the centre of the orbs forming into slits. Scales protruded, and raced across his neck, jawline and face. His glow changed from golden to an entirely different colour – the same one as her blood, and the apple.

He shook his head to rid the change, but couldn't. "I can't control—"

"Ssshhh." Eve sealed his mouth with hers, not paying any heed to the foreign feel of his tongue which had split in two like before. No monster could hide her angel from her. "There is no need to control." In fact, the brewing tempest within her was telling her the very opposite. "Deeper ... Lucifer ... I need you more."

And she wished she had words to convey her yearning. Perhaps it was the gift of angels to simply know the unknowable, but Lucifer knew her unspoken self and always had.

*Her back met grass as she was brought down to the ground, and she gasped at the prickly sensation, her skin sensitised to every little thing.*

*Lucifer leant over her, still in her; levered by his arms, hands twisted in her hair.*

*In her, but* not deep enough. *Some bottomless part of her needed him imprinted in her very soul; needed him forever.*

*She drew her legs up and around him, trying to make her craving a reality.*

*He groaned against her neck, sinking, sinking, and* finally *some cosmic key clicked into place.*

*A cry left her lips. The touch of pain was washed away by a tide of pleasure too great to escape. Everything in her tightened; clenched around both him and the tide to keep either from leaving again.*

*He felt it too. Must have done, for his soft groans became coarse sounds of pleading as he suddenly jerked and bore his whole weight down on her. A hand locked one of her legs in place, open, and he drove his whole self into her, again, and again, and again, and again, until she was the angel. She was the one flying. She was the Goddess of the world he had given her.*

*As his beautiful warmth flooded her, she gazed at the sky, and all she could see were his newly formed wings and his blood-glow ... and her identity.*

# XI
## *Home*

**H**e blinked his eyes open, feeling like he was waking from the longest sleep of his life.

The first feeling was confusion, but it was muted by elation. All his senses told him he was home.

He lifted his head from Eve's breast, and found the source of his confusion when he spied her blood covering them both from the waist down. Everything he'd ever known disappeared for a fraction of one horrendous second before he was able to separate past and present.

He'd woken up like this before and the world had gone to Hell. Literally.

But that was then, and this was now. He'd just come from Hell, and this was Heaven.

He let out a long sigh and sank back into her chest, searching for her heartbeat.

There it was.

Her fingers ruffled his hair, lightly, and he had never known contentment until this moment. Never.

"I was never allowed to forget," she said, quietly.

He stroked the side of her breast with the tip of his nose, then kissed it before settling back into her softness.

"Not an immortal being, I have lived a hundred thousand lives, reincarnated, and always Eve, or Evie, or Evangeline, or

Eva – Ava, Evvie, Eveline, Yeva, Hava, Evelia, Evita... Life.

"I never remember during my childhood years. I'm born innocent, until my first bleed, whenever that might be, and then I remember everything. It's like falling all over again – the heaviness, the pain, and of course, the weight of all the memories ... missing you; missing a part of me."

"Is that why I could never find you though I scoured every continent a hundred times over? You were never in one life long enough?"

"Perhaps. Or perhaps you were simply not allowed to. God said you would fall alone, and that you *would* forget. I never knew if you remembered me."

"I remembered," he said, firmly, "because of the apple. You saved me with that apple, and although God might have wished all knowledge taken from me, the fruit fed most of my memories of you, and some of what took place between us, although there are gaps I have never been able to fill no matter how many damn apples I eat. And I was not alone. Morgana took me under her care, so to speak, and midwifed me into my new life."

"The fairy queen?"

"Yes."

Eve fell silent, until he could take the silence no more. "Eve?"

"When sin became named, the first sin was lust. I shared it with you, and it was all we got to share. Forgive me, Lucifer – I am at this moment warring with envy."

He pulled himself up her body and met her lips with his, and then her eyes with his own. "Never – not once since you were created – have you been out of my mind."

She smiled a small smile. "Nor you, out of mine."

He kissed her again, wondering how he could even have lasted as long as he had without her touch to ignite his every cell.

"Lucifer ... shall I tell you more? About after I fell. Would you like to know?"

"Always. I've always wanted to know everything about you."

"Very well... Everything would always change after my first bleed, in any and every lifetime, with the knowledge of all that came before. How do you carry on, knowing all you thought of as truth, is a lie? Knowing the story you had lived up until that point is now meaningless in the midst of the greatest story of all that began when the Earth itself took its first breath?" She searched out his eyes with hers, a stony sincerity settling into them. "I did not lie to you, Lucifer." Eve turned her head and he followed her gaze.

Her white, Edwardian house stood nestled between others in the distance, in the same street he'd been found in, but through new eyes, the image ended right there, framed by the blurred edges of reality. Clouds still gathered over that framed existence. It still rained over mankind.

Outside of that picture, where they now lay, it was exactly as Eden had been before it fell to become Earth. The greenest grass and the grandest trees grew under twin suns that shone without hindrance. He wasn't sure how she was doing it, but like Father, like daughter – she had always been a creator in her own right. That aspect of her had fascinated him from the very beginning: that perhaps humans had the power to create where angels could not.

"That really was my life in this reincarnation. I did have adopted parents who died in a plane crash. Nothing I told you was false. But I did not bleed this time – not in this life – until yesterday. And yesterday, my reality became distorted as the same ancient memories reshaped it once more. Now, I remember it all as I always do after the first bleed.

"But there is a difference this time, Lucifer. A monumental

difference."

He waited, listening.

"The serpent finally found its wings."

He brought his head back down to her chest and kissed along the valley of her breasts. "The Dragon. Yes... I knew. Somehow, I knew the rise of the Dragon might lead me back to you."

She looked down at him, smiling sadly. "Yes." There were those slender fingers running through his hair again. Pure bliss. "Do you remember what happened between then, and when I found you outside my house?"

A cloud passed over a sun and cast a shadow across them.

He frowned, only now properly realising ten full years had passed in *her* time, since he had forfeited freedom and chased after her through the bowels of the Earth. For him, it had been less than ten days. "I do not."

"The same thing that happened to all angels, my love."

He stilled, feeling the chill of December for the first time – if it was, indeed, December.

He shook his head at her. "No, Eve. All angels lost their immortality and died that day the quakes began."

"Yes. And a new era rose. It is truly man's world now."

"I left it all behind to come and find you."

Her smile widened, no less sorrowful. A tear slipped down her cheek and pooled in the corner of her upturned lips. "And you did find me. Thank you for coming. But Lucifer ... all angels died that day. All angels." Her gaze didn't falter, her expression grave.

He slowly shook his head. "At the hospital ... I experienced things, saw things, I ... there was a woman. She was dying. She—"

"She was a part of me, as was the other. All women are a part of me."

"No. The doctors, the nurses—"

"I know them. I know them all. What you saw, you saw through my eyes."

Lucifer stared at her, bewildered. Through *her* eyes?

He looked back at the house, then at their surreal surroundings, and then, back at the beautiful being lying beneath him. "The empty streets, the lack of people..."

"Empty because I don't see people anymore." Her gaze lost its focus; her tone became detached. "Because I don't belong here anymore," she added, softly.

But he was still battling with the unforgiving, stark truth. "I'm ... dead?"

Her attention came back to him. "Yes, my angel. You're dead."

Cold clung to him, unmerciful. "If I'm dead, then ... what is this place? Where are we? Where have you brought us?"

Eve blinked and another tear fell to join the last. "Something happened to me when the serpent found its wings ten years ago. I believe I am no longer tied to this world. But this is still *Adam's* world and I am bound to Adam, therefore, trapped. I am ... half-dead."

He'd seen some horrific, terrible things in his time. He'd seen the depravity of the human mind and how dark it could go – had even pushed people to venture there for the sake of their budding clarity and potential evolution – but to hear this woman he knew to be a beacon of brightness refer to herself as 'half-dead' kindled a dread he'd not felt in a while. "Half-dead?" He pulled up, away from her, and sat.

She followed suit, still staring at him, and nodded, slowly. "Hanging on by just a thread. The thread led me straight to you. So many times in all my lives I have called your name, prayed to you, *screamed* for you hoping you'd hear me, and because the serpent found its wings and shook the Earth awake, I was finally set free from my body, and my soul travelled straight to you. Only, I had no memory of me or us then. That's why I ran – I became scared, and I ran. It is my blessing that you saw me when you did. I no longer belong here – I've never belonged here. I am bound to Adam only by bone, but you have always been my wings. I belong with you."

"And I belong with you," he said, full of certainty at that – the only sliver of certainty he felt at this moment. He had always belonged to her; had *never* stopped searching for her. Tears blurred his vision. "I thought you and Adam—"

"Sssshhh – no, no... Never Adam. Never by choice." She reached up for his face; rested her fingertips on his cheek. "Lucifer ... I need you to release me from Adam, and set me free. Stop the cycle. Arrest my next reincarnation. Please..." She glanced at her house. "I still exist as Evie, somewhere over there, but I don't have long left, and I don't want to be here anymore. Take me with you when you go."

His mind boggled as he tried to understand everything she was saying. The hallucinations he'd had, the falling apples... *Through her eyes.*

Jesus ... he thought he'd woken up in his own madness. He had woken up in hers.

"Eve," he pressed, his tone low and hard. He pulled her hand down from his face and held it on his lap. "Where is 'here'? Where are we?"

She paused too long for his liking, trying to conjure up the words she needed. "Purgatory, Lucifer. Earth is my purgatory and always has been."

Three seconds lasted an eternity, and then Lucifer growled, anger rising.

She winced as he gripped her hand too tightly.

"You have no need of *purgatory*," he spat out. "You're beyond purgatory, the place where sin swallows souls. You've committed no wrong; you've carried no crime—"

"I have, I have ... so many wrongs that I shed the blood of three billion women every month so *they* don't have to carry the memory of my fall."

"*Our* fall, and I would fall again if it meant your absolution."

She sucked in a breath. "Do you mean that? Would you fall again for all of us?"

"I mean everything I say, and you are *one* woman, Eve – one wom—"

"I'm *every* woman!" she belted out in fury, rising to her feet, sweeping both arms across the horizon. "I birthed the entire world, and in this duality every boy became Adam and every girl became Eve, whether they wanted to or not – no consent, no choice – and I *feel* every cord that binds womb to womb because their blood is *my* blood. I'm *every* woman: tall, short, big, small, black, white, yellow, red, shy and timid, bold and outspoken, but *SSSHHHHH!* Don't speak too loud or you might get broken. Back straight, head high, be confident, but meek; be on show, but let the curtain hide you; be the saint in public, sin behind closed doors; be my dare, be my temptress, but deliver me from temptation so I can do no wrong. Be *strong*, be *individual*, but hush, hush, hush, never be yourself too much, because you were made to be Eve – *just* Eve – shackled to Adam forever and ever, a*men*." A laugh ripped through her being; ripped through his. "Have you ever heard my story told separately from Adam's? *Ever?* It never has. It's always Adam *and* Eve, *their* fall, I've never been *alive* in my *own* right."

Lucifer stood, reaching for her, tears stinging his eyes at her suffering.

She turned away. "And the sons of Adam and the daughters of Eve really would have lived happily ever after, if their narrator wasn't so unreliable."

"Eve..."

"I have a confession," she said, her tone flat.

He froze at the sound of it, unsure of what to say or do to extinguish her pain.

"But surely you must already know... *Don't* you know, Lucifer?" Arms crossed over her chest, she turned back to face him, searching out his face. "I know angels must drink blood to survive in their early days fallen. Have you not tasted it in the blood of mankind when you fed?"

"I have never fed from man."

She paused, looking surprised, perhaps not having expected that answer. "So many tales of you tell of—"

"Stories, twisted to suit the teller and the audience. Let people believe what they want. I drank from animals, yes. Many animals. And I ate apple after apple to take the edge off my thirst, but I never drank from man."

"You resisted."

"Of course."

"Why? No other angel—"

"Because of *you.*"

She blinked, releasing tears.

"People are of *your* blood – how could I? Your blood is sacred, it's not food." He paused, hesitating, clearly anguished.

"Tell me," she urged.

He shuddered out a breath and looked skywards. "When we fell, I found myself landing, so to speak, in a time well after yours. The Earth was already thrumming with people. Just like how ten years have passed here, even though for me it was only a week ago that I chased you through the quakes, thousands of years passed between us when we fell. I lusted after blood, just as all angels do when they fall, but the thought of drinking from man horrified me, because I could still taste *your* blood in my mouth – feel it in my veins – *you* are human, and I could not bring myself to do it. I deteriorated fast. Fed on countless animals to no avail. Then, one day, somewhere near Jerusalem if I recall rightly, I came across a young man, tortured for having been found sleeping with his brother's son. He'd been castrated and all his limbs hacked off. Just a stump with a head, he had been left to die under the blistering sun – food for vultures and desert varmints.

"All his inner-demons were as exposed as he – shame, revulsion, humiliation – such agony. The serpent in me fed on it all, and I found that while the angel in me lusted after human blood, the snake in me lusted after human degradation. So I let it. Because the snake's lust for a man's sin-shedding quenched my thirst for blood. That's how I survived, but it became something of an addiction. Eating apples would ease it, but only for a short while, and then I would need to seek yet more depravities of humanity to keep my blood-lust from rising."

He couldn't look at her, the monster in him finally out of its cage. This is what he was.

She placed a gentle hand on his chest. He could smell her tears in the air. "You chose self-destruction over drinking the blood of mankind? Because they shared my blood? You did this for me?"

"Don't you know what you mean to me?" he choked out. He finally looked down at her, and took her face in his hands. "We only shared one moment, but if you think all it was was lust, you're a fool – I loved you. What I expressed for you with my flesh-and-bone body was *love*. I loved you before the word for love existed, and I still do."

She stared at him for an age, a thousand thoughts in her watery eyes. "Lucifer..." She mouthed his name, no sound leaving her lips.

He leaned down and kissed them.

This was completeness – her lips, her kiss, her soul on her breath... It satiated him more than any fruit, vein or sin ever could.

"Lucifer," she said again, whispering his name this time as she pulled back to meet his eyes, "you are exonerated."

"No."

"Yes. Amidst man's darkness, you may have found your drug, but you never left them there alone. You always sought to help them. To be their unseen beacon in their hour of need, despite all they say about you; what they call you – monster, demon, devil..."

"I see more than they see. At the crux of their darkness, there is potential; possibility; I see everything they can be. I see their light. At the end of all things, when the soul is left bare, the most inspiring choices are made with love, and purity of will. Those are the moments in which sin is purged, and true freedom is found."

"Adam never did see that – that light in mankind. Couldn't. He never swallowed the apple I offered to ease the pain of the fall I caused him. Instead, it caught in his throat, and he threw it back up – our cure was his poison. So, where you and I can see light *within* darkness, Adam only saw darkness. As far as he knew, light only belonged to God, so he did everything in His name; put Him on a pedestal and built temples to reach Him. It wasn't Adam's fault, but his blindness, and that of his lineage, sparked anger, and hatred, and fear ... and war." She stroked his skin above his heart. "My confession ... I've never said a word; never told a soul... Don't you know why *you* – not Adam – were the one able to see humanity's light? Why that light exists within them in the first place?"

His head began to pound. "I'm ... an angel." His mouth suddenly went dry. "Angels can see what—"

"Oh, Lucifer."

His words faded.

She leaned her head against his chest. His arms came up around her, automatically.

"Look up, Lucifer," she said, quietly.

He did, not sure what he needed to be looking for.

"Everything on Earth became a physical manifestation of all that was in Eden – this is something we both know."

"Yes," he uttered, the single word sounding hoarse. Something roared through his system, the edge of a great clarity not yet realised, pushing against all his boundaries.

"What do you see?" she pressed.

He swallowed the lump in his throat and let out a shuddering breath as he scoured the sky. "Um ... I see twin suns."

He felt her clasp his hand with hers.

She opened it until his fingers were spread wide, and then brought his palm down and rested it against her womb.

That roar crescendoed, truth dawned, and perhaps the Earth was still breaking, for that roar in his ears sounded like the end of the world all over again.

There it was.

The last thing he didn't know, he now knew.

"Yes, my angel. Twin sons. My first born were yours."

~*~

Lucifer stood there for an age, dumbfounded, as Eve watched all the pieces fall into place for him, and for them both – finally – after so long.

A great weight lifted from her at the unburdening of the greatest secret never told, which only he could be privy to – that she'd never been allowed to tell – even as she silently wept for his sorrow at never knowing his part in the growth of a race he had not once given up on; had always aided, unacknowledged.

Words evaded him. He shook his head, clearly shocked, as history sank in. *His* story.

She tightened her hold on him in an attempt to ease his shaking. "Cain and Abel ... they were both so much like you – especially Cain with his height, strength and steel – their parentage could not be denied, though Adam said nothing about it."

A small sound wormed its way out of him, followed by another, until he managed to speak. "Angels can't ... we can't procreate. We can't *create*."

"I bit the fruit of life, and you..." she let her gaze pass over the scales that still formed in patches across his arms; his neck, "you were bitten. You are not *just* an angel. Angels can't create, but you and I, together, can. We did."

His knees gave way and he fell onto them, his wide-eyed stare darting across the bloody swell of her navel, understanding setting them in a hardness she wished she could diminish.

"But duality plays cruel tricks. While Abel inherited all the light of Eden, Cain was taxed with all the darkness from the forbidden side of The Boundary. I was the only one who could see his light – so faint, but still there. Poor Cain ... he *was* good, Lucifer, he was, but so lost, and so 'angel' in his make-up he could not function well in this world made for man. Abel thrived, though; instinctively understanding the land and how to harvest the fruit of all its labour. The creator in me, was in Abel, too.

"Cain would embody all the seven sins; be the first to express man's vices. He would draw all men to recognise their own darkness through his actions. He was the mirror for all generations to come, his murder of his twin – his other half – a forever-shadow that set the destiny of humanity in stone, ensuring they would never find that missing piece of themselves they sought – mankind would never find their completion. At least, not easily. Cain is every man and woman you couldn't save in their hour of need."

Her words hit the ground; hit home. Her fingers traced his forehead, lightly, and Lucifer crumpled under their touch.

He collapsed against her womb and wept with angry loss, a fierce grieving taking place for what should have been, but never was.

"I'm so sorry," she said, her own voice breaking over his sobs. "But I did tell you – I did – every night before sleep as all my memories threatened to drown me... I told you of your children, and how I missed you, and how I wished you could see what we birthed *together,* and watch them fall and stand, and fall and stand, and try to fly..." she choked out a laugh. "I have often heard people throughout the ages talk of 'flying dreams' – dreams so real they would wake with a smile and swear they really *had* flown – and I longed to tell them they were dreaming of their father's wings, handed down to them by birthright; they just couldn't see them."

She ran a hand along his feathers, and Lucifer's body trembled in her arms, his tears trickling down her right thigh.

She held him for minutes, and every eternity that held each minute together, until he finally grew silent.

"My angel ... I love you, too, and always have."

The twin suns shone their warmth on them.

Eden had always been her favourite place, but her manifestation of Eden in this strange in-between was the temporary comfort of a past, and not an actuality.

*In between.*

She was caught in between two realities – as was Lucifer – one ending at last, and one yet to begin; one known, and one unknown. She was ready to go; to leave her children behind to stand on their own two feet, however their story may end.

With a sigh of relief at the release of her age-old confession, Eve surrendered all sin – both placed and misplaced – over the many millennia she had seen, her purgatory complete. This was Lucifer's gift, even if he didn't know it: he held the soul in a safe haven as it shed all its guise. Some didn't like it, feeling forced into facing all their ills, and her poor angel had borne the brunt of that human fear for as long as she had borne the brunt of mankind suffering for it.

Eve traced his lips with her fingertips.

He kissed one of her fingers, and she slipped it into his mouth, relishing in this closeness of each other they were wrenched from. "Do you carry the snake's poison, my love?"

Lucifer looked up at her, eyes red with tears; then with a hiss, he bared his fangs.

His dark beauty stole her breath away.

"I do. And I know what you're about to ask of me." His tears spilled, and he looked at her, torn. "And of all the things I've done in my entire existence, this will be the hardest."

She dropped to her knees in front of him. "Sometimes you have to be cruel to be kind – you know that."

Something passed over the suns and they looked up to see a flock of doves – dozens flying as one.

"M'angeal," she spoke, in their native tongue, bringing them back to the very beginning... "Ma'aith lio'baile dul." *I want to go home.* "Tóg le dul ma'baile." *Take me home.*

# XII
## The Beginning

Let me tell you a secret...

When the son of Adam and the daughter of Eve make love,
he looks upon her face and seeks himself; she looks upon
the skies and seeks her angel. Neither seeks the other. And
so it has been since the beginning.

I have been a mother for too long to count.

I have birthed dynasties; watched my children climb
heights even angels feared to conquer, and plunge into
deprivation so heinous, new paths were carved through
darkness. And all I could do was watch.

I have been maiden, mother and crone – alone – bled
over entire cities; washed, rinsed and repeated it all in a
cycle I refused to break, lest my children break. That's
what mothers do – hold everything together.

But I have been breaking in their place.

I have lived every life except my own.

There is one thing I long to experience once more:
Oneness. Unity.

Created incomplete – as perhaps we all are under duality's reign – in my angel's arms is the only place I have ever known oneness, and embedded in the expanse of time, I lived it only for the smallest fraction of the smallest second.

But I have remembered it: have never been allowed to forget it – my memories, every incarnation, stripping me of hope and second chances because nothing can compare to the peace found in wholeness.

Loneliness is a black hole.

I have been lonely for so long, acknowledged, but not seen: heard, but not listened to.

I do not know who I am outside of the thoughts of my children. Who is a mother when not a mother? One cannot 'undo' birth. Once a mother, always a mother. I can never go back to who I was before. I can only go on.

For the first time since I sank my teeth into the flesh of a red fruit, I have choice again. And when we are given a gift, we must share it. Maybe, by letting go of my children, I am also sharing this new gift. Maybe when I leave, they will have choice.

Adam and I parted ways a long time ago. In truth, we have only ever gotten on with an awkward acceptance of the other's plight. Made from his bone, I have always lived under his unintended asylum, and what man is ever agreeable towards the woman he is tied to: made to temper him: made to keep him from fulfilling his wildest passions?

Our circumstances being what they were, Adam has always regarded women with suspicion and caution; occasionally with fear. He has always preferred the company of men, and thus, is a great leader of men.

But Adam still holds on to ... the idea of me. Just as Father did. No child should have to live and grow in the shadow of someone's idea, yet from the moment they enter this world they are labelled – boy, girl – and a subconscious expectation is set. It is my fault. I was the first 'ideal' of what women should be and what men should admire. When I am gone, and no longer bleeding for the world, perhaps they will know who they truly are. Perhaps they will finally have their identity.

I am scared.

I don't know who I am.

The thought of being whoever I want is a terrifying thing, because I have only ever been who everyone has wanted me to be.

Lucifer is the only one who has never placed any expectation on my being. Do I get to be with him now? I do not know the answer. I do not know what comes after this. It is a secret for the next who carries Genesis, and the next who brings the New Dawn.

It is fitting that my angel, of all beings, should be the one to set me free – he has freed so many before me, but I hope in freeing me, he is able to free himself, too. I wish you had all known him before his fall; before he was hidden from sight by scales and hardened by hurt. He was a star – a golden star with a golden heart that set love alight across the skies of Heaven before the word 'love' existed. Some of you still carry his blood in your veins, and he fathered you many a time during your blackest hours, unbeknownst to both you and him.

In a short while, I shall pull my hair back from my neck and offer Lucifer my vein to receive his venom, and I wonder if I shall ever see you, my children, again. I wonder what I will become. One thing placates my fear: the knowledge that, although I don't know who I am, I have been every woman.

I have had the privilege of knowing both the best and worst of souls. I have lived within the strongest of hearts and the brightest of minds. I am every woman. I am every woman. I am every woman. I am every woman. I am every woman. I am every woman. I am every woman. I am every woman. I am every woman. I am every woman. I am every woman. I am every woman. I am every woman. I am every woman. I am every woman. I am every woman. I am every woman. I am every woman. I am every woman. I am every woman. I am every woman. I am every woman. I am every woman. I am every woman. I am every woman. I am every woman. I am every woman. I am every woman. I am every woman. I am every woman. I am every woman. I am every woman. I am every woman. I am every woman. I am every woman. I am every woman. I am every woman...

Mark Strobel jumped out of his skin at the loud ringing of his phone, the harsh sound of it hurtling around the room, almost as loudly as the rain drummed against the window pane.

Private number.

"Dr Strobel," he answered, his heart going at the rate of knots. He'd been immersed in her words.

He put down Evie's notebook on the small table in the corner of her room, next to her makeshift bookmark: a post-card of John Collier's *Lilith*. Next to the name *Lilith* she had drawn a question mark, and she had underscored the name with a wavy line. Knowing the full contents of Evie's notebook, Mark had to smile at that.

"Are you with her?" came the voice at the other end.

He let out a sigh of irritation under his breath. Philip Reem always kept his number private, so it wasn't exactly easy to tell if it was him at the other end. "Yes. You got the phone call, too, I take it."

"Yes, I've just entered reception downstairs. Will be up in five. Nurse Rankin in today?"

"It's Christmas Day, Philip – almost no one's in."

Philip snorted and Mark hung up, annoyed at his colleague's intrusion into his reverie.

Or was it Evie's reverie?

He sighed again, this time in sorrow as he looked back at the colossal notebook, and then let his gaze fall on the woman who had been his and Philip's patient for a decade.

He strode towards where she lay on her bed, and pulled up a chair so he was level with her. His heart squeezed at the ties binding her wrists to the bed railings – there so she wouldn't hurt herself. She didn't normally need the restraints, but they had received the call this morning to saying she'd had a seizure – had almost knocked herself out because of it – and they didn't yet know the cause. She had never had a seizure before, and this one was accompanied by one hell of an anomaly.

He stared at the blood stains on her gown, disgusted that

the staff hadn't bothered to change her yet. He'd be having words with them about that.

She'd started menstruating. And since she'd been diagnosed with primary amenorrhoea back in her teens, they were stumped at the medical reason for the onset now. He could currently only theorise that the seizure, and the start of her menses, were somehow related.

"Evie?" he called out.

No response.

Her blonde hair matted to the sides of her head, and her open blue eyes didn't even flicker. No change there, though. Occasionally, there was a spark of something, but it was rare.

She hadn't said a single word since the plane crash ten years ago when she'd first been brought into St Mary's Hospital. Her survival of the crash had been so miraculous, they had nick-named her 'Lucky' before they had confirmation of her real name.

Suffering the loss of her parents, a hazardous blow to the left side of her head, a shattered left knee and a nasty sprain to her wrist – not to mention the trauma of the crash itself – it had soon become clear she was emotionally and psychologic-ally damaged, even though her physical recovery had pro-ceeded better than expected.

She had no living relatives to support her, and she had never given any indication she even remembered being on the plane, preferring to draw diagrams of black holes and write tales of dragons and earthquakes, instead.

Over the years observing her, he had come to suspect it was guilt that kept her from putting herself on that plane again – the belief that she should not have lived when all others had died, causing a complete denial of her inclusion in the event. A voluntary amnesia of the way it had all played out. Forgetting must be heaven; remembering was no doubt hell.

Dr Reem and himself had been called in as part of the hospital's liaison psychiatry team. After six months, she'd been transferred to the Adamson Wing of the hospital as a mental inpatient, and here she had stayed.

Though no words came out of her mouth, she was full of words, and she wrote them all down.

He glanced once more at the five hundred page notebook he'd left on the table.

*Amazing words.*

He looked back at her, trying to find any small sign of life, bar her breathing. "Evie, can you hear me?"

Silence.

"You don't have to shut everyone out, you know."

The door swung open and in walked Philip.

Whereas Mark was the clinical psychologist primarily concerned with healing through interpersonal approaches, Philip – one of the country's leading psychiatrists – took a more cold stance, looking mainly for behavioural patterns caused by chemical imbalances, and treating patients via medication.

More often than not, they didn't get on, neither really understanding the way the other worked, but they did hold a grudging respect for the other's expertise in their own field, and they had one thing in common: the extraordinariness that was Evie.

"Merry Christmas," nodded Philip.

"And to you."

"How's she been."

"Same as usual."

"Unresponsive?"

"Pretty much, although there's a new entry in her notebook. Presumably she wrote it before the seizure."

Philip raised an eyebrow at him, got out his pen light and proceeded with his examination of Evie, flashing the light into her pupils. "I've said time and time again, that notebook of hers is little more than a good yarn – all fiction, no fact. Everything she writes is fantasy – at best, theory – not reality, and it doesn't help with our diagnoses of her, or her progression back into the world."

"It's fascinating – every single word is fascinating. Some of it's close to genius. It's a portal into her mind."

"A broken mind."

"You should read it."

"I have."

"Read the recent entries."

"Stories, Mark. In which she is a parent – the creator of human beings, no less – this coming from a woman who never knew her real parents, lost her adopted ones, and was told she might never have children." He frowned at the blood on her gown. "I read about the onset of her menses in her notes just now," he muttered, clearly frustrated at not having an answer for it.

"I think it's interesting she wrote about her menstruation. The last few pages were on that – her bleeding for the first time. You really should read it."

"Does she write about her electrolyte balance?" he asked, dryly.

Mark crossed his arms. "Well, you're missing a treat."

"She has a classic god complex."

Mark snorted. "That is *not* a clinical term, and not even an accurate description of what she's expressing."

Philip laughed. "I'm just playing devil's advocate. I get it – I do. I read her early scribblings. I don't need to read her recent ones to see the picture. She expresses herself through powerful, immortal beings to make up for her lack in life, perhaps even her lack of identity – she's adopted for heaven's sake, without even a surname on her birth certificate. Her stories are about humans with super powers, fallen angels finding their soul-mates, demons being redeemed – redemption's a big issue for her – magic pens that make whatever you write come true or whatnot. It's standard projection."

"I'm not denying that, but her stories are intriguing on about ten different levels. Can't you see the layers?"

He shrugged. "That's your area of expertise, not mine. Standard fiction if you ask me – minus the vampires everyone seems to like so much nowadays. My deduction is that she could have been a promising author."

"Is. And did you know *we* feature in this story of hers?"

"Yes," he mumbled, unimpressed, as he added his observations to her chart on her clipboard. "I remember the Jekyll and Hyde reference you gave me. Of course we feature. We're all she's known for ten years."

Mark bit his tongue. There was so much more than Philip was suggesting, but he was right in one respect: while Mark could add her stories to her files and make a riveting psychological case study out of them, none of it had proven any use in terms of her improvement.

Still, Philip didn't have to be such a condescending twat about it. He'd always been that way. Mark even found him that way with his patients. There was one point, about five years ago, when they had felt they'd been on the verge of coaxing Evie out of her shell, and to this day he felt Philip had pushed her too hard; demanded too much, too soon, and laid the guilt on thick when she couldn't or wouldn't comply.

Not that Philip ever saw it. Not that Philip ever thought of anything other than what was in front of his nose. As far as he was concerned, all her ails could be attributed to the crash – five percent of her brain had been damaged.

In Mark's mind, he couldn't quite equate 'brain damage' with the enticing words she wrote. All the test results showed one thing; her writing showed something entirely different.

But science answered to test results.

Philip might have an excellent reputation as a psychiatrist, but if he'd *just* read between the lines of Evie's stories...

Admittedly, Mark found her tales mesmerising on a personal level, even with his psychology hat off.

Philip threw him a look. "I've always warned you about getting too close to this one."

"I'm not close," he lied. "I'm just observant."

"Well," Philip smiled and hung her chart back up, "if it gets you that grant for your project, study her stories all you like."

Mark gritted his teeth. Yes, he'd been working himself ragged for the grant, and Evie was one of his better case studies, but that wasn't his goal with her, not that the infamous Dr Reem would appreciate that – he'd put his own mother into a home last year so he could sell her house to buy himself a bigger one without an inkling of remorse. The man had two sons and a daughter of his own – not that he mentioned them much – and Mark kinda hoped they might do the same to him one day.

"I'll tell you what *is* interesting," said Philip, changing the subject. "Both her white and red blood cell counts are down – way down – almost as if she's got severe food poisoning. There's also some dehydration. Okay, I'm going to write this up, confer with whichever doctor's doing the rounds, and leave the pharmacist and nurses instructions for administering some immediate medication. I'll book a CT scan in for her for tomorrow – I'll be lucky to get anything to happen today. You staying, or going?"

"Allison went into labour at five this morning, over at St George's, so I won't be staying too much longer."

"She your eldest?"

"She is."

"Your first grandchild on the way?"

"Yep." Making him a fairly young grandfather, since Allison was only twenty, but she had been adamant about keeping the baby, and her boyfriend seemed committed enough. Allison had always had her head screwed on, so he trusted her judgement. It's not as if he wouldn't be there for her. He was her father. He wasn't going to leave her in her hour of need.

"Hmmm ... the best thing about the little cherubs is you get to give them back," he grinned.

Mark forced a smile.

Philip saluted him. "Later, Dr Strobel."

"Indeed." *Much later.*

Philip shut the door behind him and Mark rose from his chair, feeling somewhat uneasy. It was the mention of Allison. He'd wanted to be at the hospital with her and everyone else, but he'd been called in here, which of course, was also important, but his daughter...

It wasn't like there was anything left to do here – they had all the bases covered.

He grabbed his coat and scarf from where he'd left them, on the arm of the other chair, and put them on, then went to retrieve Evie's notebook from the table to place it back where she liked to keep it, under her mattress.

Evie was staring at him.

He started, caught off-guard, and the book slipped from his grasp, landing on the floor, the *Lilith* postcard flying out of it. "Jesus fucking Christ..."

Her blue eyes were fixed on his, and over the goosebumps racing all over his body, he finally realised they were *aware*, not glazed over like usual.

"Evie...?"

Hesitantly, he took a couple of steps towards her, unnerved as hell, which was daft, but he couldn't help it. The way she looked at him, it was ... like she *saw* him.

"Evie, can you hear me?"

He stopped all movement when he got a response. Her lips curved up, so very slowly, into a smile.

His phone caterwauled its ringing tone once more, and this time he all but shouted his curse as he reached into his pocket for it. He really had to change its fucking tune.

The screen read **Allison**.

*God, it's Allison.*

Fear tightened around his throat that the news might be bad, and he was torn. He needed to answer this, but his usually unresponsive patient of ten years had suddenly made a break-through.

*Fuck.*

Heart won over duty. "Don't ... move," he said, stupidly, to Evie, who still stared at him, smiling, and really, he was an idiot because she wasn't going anywhere with those restraints.

He answered his phone. "Allison, honey..."

"Daddy?"

"Baby, you okay?"

He heard a sob at the other end. He was close to sprinting out of there. "Allison?"

"Girls," she cried, at the other end.

"Gir—what?"

She let out a small laugh which eased his clenched heart. "Twin girls. No one knew – one was behind the other." Her laughter tripped over small sobs of joy. "I have twin girls. They're wonderful. We're all good."

"Allie..." He welled up, relief showering over him. The sun beamed into the room, and for a second, all he could see were gold and red hues through his lashes. He blinked and turned his head a little, faintly registering that it had been a while since he'd seen the sun – it had been such a cold, wet winter.

"Oh, honey, congratulations. I don't know what to say – I'm so, so happy."

"Me, too. Thanks. Are you coming by soon?"

"God, yes. I wish I'd been there."

"It's okay. Steven and Mum have been great."

"Good. I'm just leaving work now. I'm going to be as quick as I can." For some reason he couldn't fathom, his voice broke, a strange sense of urgency taking over all else, perhaps because he hadn't been there when he should have been.

A horn beeped from outside, and he stepped forward and looked out the window to see a truck driver starting an argument with a van driver. The sliding billboard behind the truck moved, advertising some kind of perfume or something, with a slogan – half obscured by the vehicle – that set off a tune in his head to some old track his mother used to listen to: ***It's a man's world, but it would be nothing without—***

"Okay, Dad, I'll see you soon."

"Wait! Allie..."

He snapped out of his daze, and his gaze fell on the notebook on the floor. He frowned when he noticed a couple of the pages had been crumpled by the fall.

"Yeah?"

He paused, not sure what he needed to say, but feeling the need to say something nonetheless. He focused on the suspended specks of dust caught in the light of the sun. "This is just the beginning, you know that, right? I mean, *your* beginning."

"Um—"

"No, I mean ... you can be anything you want to be. Anything. Anyone. You're a mother now, and I'm so goddamned proud of you, but you're also everything you were before, and everything you'll still become – the whole world is yours and don't you let anyone ever tell you otherwise. And we'll make sure to teach your girls the same."

Heavy silence greeted him.

So ... that sucked. He wasn't so good with the words. He rolled his eyes at himself.

Allison giggled at the other end. "Dad, have you been on the Buck's Fizz already?"

He smiled. "That might have come out better if I had been, huh?"

More giggling.

"Okay, I'm, er ... gonna hang up now and make my way to you."

"Wait ... Daddy?"

"Yeah?"

"I love you."

Fucking tears. He couldn't walk out of here with red eyes. "I love you, too, honey. See you soon."

"See ya."

He hung up, feeling both exhausted and better. She was okay. The birth went smoothly, and she was okay.

He turned back to Evie, and froze.

He knew it without touching her.

The stillness.

The slight smoothness to her skin which had not been there two minutes ago.

"No..."

What had happened?

"Shit, no..."

He'd been facing the other way, looking towards the window, but he hadn't heard her make a sound. Surely there hadn't been another seizure?

"Fuck..."

It seemed she'd gone peacefully.

Her eyes were now closed, but that small smile still graced her features.

Maybe he had it wrong.

Her chest didn't move, not even a little bit.

With effort, he managed to work his feet until he was standing by her side. Carefully, he pressed two fingers into her left wrist, more than annoyed at the strap he had to move out the way, feeling for a pulse.

There wasn't one.

He should do something – go get someone. They would perform CPR; try to save her.

*She's ready to go ... she doesn't want to be saved.*

He wasn't qualified to call it.

Fuck it, he'd lose his job if he didn't *move* his damn self.

With his heart hurting, he reached for the call button on the small remote hanging off the side of the bed and pressed it.

"Fuck it, Evie," he whispered, his voice thick. "This had better be what you wanted."

Something shimmered in his peripheral vision.

He turned back towards the window and saw what it was.

A small, fluffy feather, probably escaped from Evie's pillow, floated in the air, gently making its way towards the floor. It was white, but the sun's rays tinted it gold and a pinky-red, depending on the angle it turned. It landed on Evie's notebook.

With a sad smile, he bent down and picked the book up.

He straightened the crumpled pages as best as he could as he waited for the staff, and then shut the thick notebook, only to have the heavy back cover fall open again.

It was then that he caught the words he hadn't seen before.

He thought she'd ended her entry with the last thing he'd read, three quarters of the way through the book, because every other leaf from there until the last one, was blank.

He looked at Evie, blinked back fresh tears, and then looked back at her words. He traced over them with his fingers, across the back page, and silently wished her goodbye before closing the book for good, just as the door to the room opened.

*And every woman is me.*

# Acknowledgements

Who do I thank? I suppose I should thank Lucifer – no, seriously – because I had no idea how this story was going to be going in. Actually, that's not true: I knew *exactly* how this story was going to be going in, but I had no idea I would be so wrong. So very wrong.

I wanted to write a story about Lucifer; Lucifer told me, unequivocally, that I would NOT be writing a story about him at all – I would be writing a story about "Saving Eve". About women. About society. And in writing that I would discover his story, or at least a shade of it, because, he told me, he is a shadow – a shadow that gives depth to all light. A shadow, alone, can never be understood, but study the light and you will see everything the shadow has to offer.

As you can see, I had many interesting (frustrating) conversations with Lucifer whilst trying to pen this book.

But I thank him. You hear that, Lucifer? "Thank you!"

Additional and heartfelt thanks to Ninfa Hayes, Elizabeth Morgan, Amanda L. Pederick, the entire Satin Smoke Press Room, and – never least – my beautiful family for understanding the processes I need to go through when I write, even when I barely understand them myself. I love you.

Dianna Hardy
10th April, 2015

## *Also by Dianna Hardy*

# The Spell of Summer
## (Once Times Thrice)

CONTEMPORARY ROMANCE
WITH JUST A HINT OF MAGIC

Meredith is leading a straight-laced life in London with her straight-laced fiancé, determined to forget her reckless, wild-child past. They're about to get married.

Jamie is an old, poetic soul with a broken heart returning home to Cornwall to get his life back in order.

### *What binds them?*

One chance meeting thirteen summers ago; one innocent spell spoken after one perfect night...

And now history is unravelling; the past and present, merging...

**Words can change everything, but can they change your destiny?**

And in the messy world of magic, what part does love play?

It's summer all over again, but the spell has only just begun.

"The Spell of Summer is possibly her best book yet..."
*Author, Elizabeth Morgan*

"...addictive and amazingly wonderful."
*The Paranormal Bookshelf*

"I was whisked away into an emotional roller coaster ride from beginning to end."
*Book Reviews by Lynn*

# Broken Lights

### GRITTY, SUSPENSEFUL ROMANCE

## *What's really worth fighting for when one second is all you have left?*

Norman Smithson is at the end of the line. His wife left him, women don't look at him, he was made redundant, and at forty, he could be just that little bit slimmer. He would be a has-been if he'd ever been a 'was' in the first place. He's not the Alpha male of the 21st century – or of any century. He was the chubby oddball who used to sit silently at the back of the class so he wouldn't get picked on.

Rosa is a dreadlocked, tattooed and pierced twenty-something, who uses her image as armour to keep everyone away from every broken thing about her. But her past is about to catch up with her ... at the exact moment Norman finds himself in completely the wrong place, at the worst possible time.

One gunshot, one scramble for life, one unlikely couple, one very long night ... can one damaged woman and one ordinary man, find the extraordinary in the very last second they're given?

"Dianna knows how to tell each and every one of her character's story as if it was her own life that she is talking about and sometimes you feel as if she has been in your own head as if you are one of the characters."
*Nancy at The Avid Reader*

"What I loved especially about this read was not only its uniqueness in the genre creating a fresh and bold read, but the strength of the characters. Norman especially was a character who was easy to fall in love with. His brokenness was endearing and his road to discovery was lovely."
*Bex 'n' Books*

"This story is about loss, hope, love, and finding that one special someone who is worth fighting for."
*Book Reviews By Lynn*

## More Titles

Eye of the Storm series
*followed by*
After the Storm novelettes
*and*
Blood Never Lies duet

'Til Death Do Us Part
(an adult retelling of The Little Mermaid)

A Silver Kiss
(Vampire Poetry)

All info can be found at:
**www.diannahardy.com**

# About The Author

Dianna Hardy is an international bestselling author of (cross-genre) fantasy fiction, most notable for her dark paranormal fantasy and the raw, intense Eye of the Storm series. But her heart-warming Once Times Thrice series proves she thrives in the light as much as the dark. Whatever your poison, what she loves most is to bring you stories that are action-packed, fast-paced and not short of heat, with the focus on character development, relationship dynamics, and the plot. She writes full-length novels and short fiction.

She currently lives in South Hampshire, UK with her partner and their daughter, where she writes full-time.

Official site:
**www.diannahardy.com**

Facebook:
**www.facebook.com/authordiannahardy**

Twitter:
**www.twitter.com/thewitchingpen**